TIME AND TIME AGAIN

HIDE THE SAUSAGE

GERRY HUERTH

LitPrime Solutions
21250 Hawthorne Blvd
Suite 500, Torrance, CA 90503
www.litprime.com
Phone: 1-800-981-9893

Published by LitPrime Solutions   05/19/2023

ISBN: 979-8-88703-240-5(sc)
ISBN: 979-8-88703-241-2(e)

Library of Congress Control Number: 2023908473

CONTENTS

"Little spirit, gentle wanderer,
Companion guest of the body,
In what place will you now abide,
Pale, stark, bare,
Unable as you used to play?"
Written by the Roman Emperor Hadrianus
(lived AD 76-138)

PROLOGUE

138 AD

In the darkness moaning breaths rasp in a rhythm of agony; then a few gasps in quick succession followed by suspenseful silence, then more gasps and silence. Vague shadows hover around a bed in that dark room. A muffled whisper disturb a period of momentary stillness, "Is he dead yet? How much longer do we need to stay?"

Another shadowy voice hisses, "Shhhhhhhhh!"

Finally the whispery gloom is broken by a desperate guttural gasp for air.

A narrow strip of daylight shines through a gap between the drawn, thick curtains, piercing the shadow and streaking across the bed in a delicate shaft that seems to bind the gasping form to the bed. Just enough light is cast to reveal the dark shifting human shapes that crowd the room.

Once, a whole empire had bowed to the wishes of that bound and helpless form; now only a roomful of impatient people hover waiting to be done with the anti-climax of the life of Emperor Hadrianus. His naked arms, once so powerful, now shriveled, lie above the covers. His left hand clutches something in a claw-like grasp; his right arm, in repetitive motion, feebly reaches to that shaft of light.

One figure, Julianus, the private secretary of Hadrianus, bustles around the room like an exasperated master of ceremonies, frantically directing the silhouetted forms crowding around the bed.

Unobtrusively a female, an ancient slave, reaches through the shaft of light to place a damp cloth on Hadrianus' forehead.

For an instant his eyes open, curious about the only figure that touches him with tenderness. Even in the shadow his eyes are still a piercing green. Then he grimaces in disappointment and starts his frantic reaching toward the light again and again.

From a dark corner of the room, the sound of a metal bowl falling to the floor gongs, the sound keeps repeating, ever diminishing as the object seeks a new equilibrium on the floor. The whispering, opaque shapes stir in confusion. One shadowy form rushes into the faint light by the bed. Pedanius, a ferret-faced, shifty-looking middle aged man, touches the arm of the dying man. "It wasn't my fault. It wasn't my fault."

Ever vigilant Julianus stares at Pedanius with withering contempt. "Shhhhhhhhhh."

Pedanius riles like a cornered rat, pointing to the old woman. It was her…that stupid slave!"

Julianus retorts smugly. "Decorim, Pedanius, decorum."

Pedanius cowers and retreats back into the shadow, whining, "He's MY uncle, after all."

Hadrianus lets out a roar of agony.

Julianus hisses at Pedanius, "Are you happy now?"

Hadrianus' hand reaches more frantically for the light.

Julianus screams at a lumbering figure at the foot of the bed. "Recite something, Babilla…quickly! Make yourself useful for once."

In a high girlish voice, the lumbering figure, complains, " I'm not ready for…"

"Anything, you fool!"

Babilla's voice now transforms; she speaks in deep masculine tones, "I sing of the arms and the man… ."

Pedanius hisses, "Just because she wears a toga, she thinks she's Virgil."

Hadrianus gasps and then splutters in rage. His left hand clutches more tightly at the object hidden by his clawed fingers.

The shadows in the room clamor in nervous panic.

The Ancient Slave Woman quietly bends over to listen to Hadrianus. She turns toward the darkened frantic audience. Though her voice is soft, it seems to have an eerie command of the room. "He wants the boy."

Julianus snaps at Babilla. "Make your self useful; get the boy!"

Babilla looks bewildered, "But he's," she whispers, "dead."

Agnes, a predatory looking older woman with violently red-dyed hair whispers to Pedanius, "The boy …" and laughs with wretched glee.

Julianus fixes his eyes on Babilla. "Get it!"

"Do you mean…?"

"Get it!"

Babilla lumbers across the room tentatively opening the large bronze doors and slips through them.

Sealed off from the room, her face relaxes as she plods down the once grand hallways, now covered in dust. With child-like curiosity she notices a pile of refuse peeking out of a corner. Ahead she hears the sounds of cackling laughter. Her pace picks up.

Sitting on the ground, four slaves huddle around a makeshift table. A young slave shouts, "I won, I won!"

An incredibly old, decrepit slave shakily puts a card on the table, cackling in satisfaction. "It's not over, until it's over. Just ask old Hadrianus." He notices Babilla and grins at her as if she were in on the joke.

At first she smiles too, then pauses assuming a dignified pose. She clears her voice and in deep dramatic tones proclaims. "You are speaking about our…the Magnificent Hadrianus!"

The decrepit slave makes a shaky motion with his hand as if brushing away a fly. "It's all right dearie. Here today, gone tomorrow." He studies her with dithering glee. "Here, again."

She glares at the slaves. "Bring in the statue!"

The young slave stands up nodding obsequiously. "His wife's?"

Babilla splutters impatiently, "No, no, no, no."

The old slave shakes his head to no one in particular. "I never thought Sabina should've married that upstart anyway." He stares accusingly at Babilla. "Dead, dead, dead."

Babilla looks flustered, pleading. "Get it…the boy."

The old slave keeps staring at her. "You were a friend of hers, weren't you?" He cackles. "A very special friend." He smiles in lewd satisfaction. "Thought you could get away with something, didn't you? Then you just left her, like everybody else."

Babilla flees down the hall in panic as all the slaves rise.

She sneaks back into the darkened room.

"Pedanius is hovering over the gasping body, declaiming. "Your name like Rome's is eternal. We, your humble servants revolve around you like the skies around the world."

Julianus yanks him away from the bed.

Agnes sidles into the space left by Pedanius. "My glorious emperor…"

Suddenly the brass double doors open; dim light exposes the room more clearly. Julianus elbows Agnes away.

Startled, Hadrianus opens his eyes.

Slaves are pulling in a life size statue. It wobbles, but with some effort is placed at the foot of the bed.

Hadrianus raves…light more light!"

In panic all the people in the room start screaming "Light, light, light!"

For a moment Julianus is lost in the confusion. Once again he composes himself. "Open the curtains, you fools!"

Suddenly splendid sunlight fills the room. The figure of a beautiful young man vividly comes to life. Hadrianus stares at the statue with wild eyed ecstasy, his whole body rocks urgently to get closer to the bright form.

Hadrianus screams, "Closer, Closer!"

The slaves frantically cart the statue to the side of the bed. Now it stands in front of Hadrianus, brilliantly lit.

Hadrianus' desperate rocking becomes more frantic.

Voices cry out around the room, "Antinous is here, he's here!"

Suddenly Hadrianus looks bewildered. Next to his bed is a cold statue. He screams, "No, no, no." Wide-eyed he gasps for air.

All the onlookers flutter around the room in a frenzy.

Julianus screams, "Get that thing out of here. Everybody out, out!"

Slaves pull the statue away as the crowd starts edging toward the door.

Pedanius complains to Agnes, "Who left him in charge? He's just a secretary, paid help. I'm of royal blood."

Agnes glances cautiously at Julianus and then whispers to Pedanius, "He'll be out of a job soon enough. He'll get what he deserves…Mr. Perfect High and Mighty."

The Ancient Slave Woman stands at the head of the bed tenderly watching Hadrianus' agony. Despite the chaos, she doesn't look away from his face.

His breath stops, his body trembles as if some internal struggle is taking place, then a horrible barking scream roars from his mask-like face. His eyes go glassy as all animation drains from his body, leaving a gruesome smile on his face.

Everyone halts to watch, frozen in time.

The Ancient Slave Woman gently closes the staring eyes of the once magnificent Hadrianus and silently departs.

Suddenly the onlookers come to life and start strolling casually out of the room.

Agnes chats to no one in particular, "I can hardly wait to get back to Rome. He took forever to die."

Julianus nervously paces back and forth by the bed until the last stragglers have left. Then he stops to gaze at the corpse with its ghoulish smile. For just an instant Julianus looks bewildered, almost sad, then his face tightens. He looks over his shoulder anxiously to see if anyone is watching. He reaches toward the tightly clasped hand of Hadrianus and desperately tries to pry it open.

Someone enters the room: the Ancient Slave Woman.

Julianus quickly jerks his hands away and slyly flees the room.

Only the Ancient Slave Woman remains. Humming, she gently places her hand on Hadrianus' desperate mask of a face; it relaxes. Even his tightly fisted left hand releases its burden. She picks up what he had been clutching so desperately. A golden bird, wings outspread, sparkles in the sun light.

CHAPTER 1

1990

Between you and me, those labyrinthine corridors of Tony's mind are not particularly well lit. Though to be absolutely fair to Tony, and fair I always am, it is not malicious intent on his part that triggers all those mishaps that spill over onto anyone in his vicinity. Outrage would be pointless, as pointless as being aghast at a puppy for urinating on the kitchen floor. Not that I am not absolutely resolute in applying just the right amount of reproach to curtail future spillage. You see, I am consistent. Certainly, especially of late, I have had ample opportunities to exercise this signature trait of mine. After all I know who is really in charge here.

To get back to Tony though, and this story is really about Tony, behind that innocent smile of his, dramatic absurdities run blind and frantic, and even I, Julian Scribner, the most innocent of men (this may sound like hubris, but I am quite confident in this self- estimation) have found myself slipping into pools of mess, not a pleasant predicament. Though I still remain undaunted in my attempts to serve as a rectifying influence, not just to the benighted Tony, but to everyone else around me; the strain IS beginning to tell. At moments I have even started suspecting that my sharp sense of purpose is being dulled.

Though to get back to the blame that I so generously am not attributing to dear Tony; lately life has been challenging, even for someone of my far from ordinary acumen. I have noticed a tilt to my world, things no longer coming together at precise right angles any more, yes, mess. Just this afternoon when I was examining my life to identify and eradicate any potential mistakes, I realized that something of the haphazard had begun seeping into my routine from that very first afternoon that I met the dear boy. What a coincidence!

Though I am careful not to mention it (after all I have a reputation to maintain), that tilting now has become so extreme that at moments my world seems absolutely askew. Though of course, I maintain my image of wise decorum. After all, no one else need know that my careful life is being bombarded by absurdities. Even my usual sleep of the just has been interrupted lately. Why, last night when I went to bed, simply wanting to enjoy the reward of a deep and dreamless sleep, I felt dizzy. Certainly it could not have been anxiety since I always finish to perfection any task I undertake, digesting my day easily. But through that stubborn night all the sounds of the city kept streaming through me: yowling sirens, a car screeching to a halt at the stop sign outside, dogs in darkened yards barking at the moon. Those sounds streamed through and took on fantastic shapes and stories in my mind determined to sleep. The world of other people's folly seemed to have a life of its own to which I was being helplessly subjected. Fortunately the clear light of morning dispelled that foolishness.

To get back to Tony, and I do not mean this as a reproach,

I remember our first meeting. That fateful moment hangs suspended like a bubble in my mind lit by the August sun that bleached those downtown streets into a noisy glare. My memory says it was three years ago, but even time now is getting distorted, and that moment seems like eons ago or perhaps tomorrow. As usual, and I can assure you that up to that point in my life I was a person of the righteously usual, I had just put some finishing touches on another of my scholarly papers on Roman law, antecedent to its being dispatched, on invitation of course, to a not unprestigious, academic journal, another of my lauded studies filled with fascinating, arcane, Roman details. Readers are always astonished at the amount of detail.

You see, in summer I am freed from the onerous burden of teaching history to university students whose minds have literally been subsumed by various and sundry electronic gadgets. We are creating a new species of human beings whose cerebral activity occurs outside of the cranium, but I will not get into that now. At any rate, in summer I can finally immerse myself in academic pursuits that are more fitting to my dignity as a tenured professor of ancient history at the University of Minnesota.

On that afternoon in August, driving home reveling in the glories of the *Edict Perpetuum*, marveling at this coup de gras to the pretense of republican Rome (I do not need to explain to you how the emperor Hadrian through this brilliant document assumed absolute command over the hitherto messy and decentralized body of Roman law, creating a legal monument so elegant and concise that I could have written it myself, a document which has had repercussions for future kings and popes and even the sympathetic Milowitz Brothers who look down from billboards all over the city under the caption, "Had an accident, call us," but I will not get into that right now) I made a wrong turn. Let me assure you, a very rare event in my life. I was innocently driving down the freeway en-route to my home and a much deserved rest. Needless to say, I am a skilled and careful driver. I had just signaled and was entering the right lane to reach the exit ramp. A souped-up old Imperial convertible sped along the highway as if it owned the road; it brutally shouldered me out of the lane. I glanced over to see the driver, a shirtless young monstrosity smiling complacently as he not only put my life at risk, but also made me miss my exit. Perhaps because I make so few mistakes, a negligible amount really, I felt a moment of bewilderment. Needless to say I expressed justifiable outrage. I took the very next exit and found myself driving through downtown Minneapolis during rush hour.

Though I normally do not let such transient forces disturb me, for a moment, the accumulated effect of glare and heat and noise were simply too much. There I was in that cauldron of a city, trapped in traffic, horns rudely blasting all around me. I was stalled in traffic. To make matters even worse, a frowzy and unkempt woman, an ancient old thing, was pushing a grocery cart full of her squalid processions across the street; in front of me. Moldy clothes, yellowish newspapers and assorted bits of revolting debris were stuffed into the cart; it was a disgusting accident waiting to happen..

To my annoyance, she seemed serenely oblivious to her pathetic condition. As she passed in front of my car, she stared at me through my car window. For an instant I almost thought that I remembered her (did I tell you that I have a perfect photographic memory?), then I realized that I was simply becoming overheated, and the heat waves rippling from the asphalt were creating a visual distortion.

She stood there with her disgusting cart, peering at me. The old idiot, obviously demented, smiled at me (there has to be some way to keep that kind of people off the street so that they do not disrupt our lives). A gust of hot wind caught one of the loose papers on her cart and sent it flapping through the air. To my dismay it landed on my windshield. Did I mention how people like her create such mess? A torn off cover of *TIME Magazine* was plastered against my windshield impeding my acute vision; the big bold letters "*TIME*" staring at me. Why, time is my orderly friend; I, Julian Scribner, manage time. I don't need it spilling out and cluttering my horizon.

And then she rolled her clattering cart past me and across the street. Just then the traffic started moving, *TIME* flew off my windshield and into the overheated chaos of the city.

Did I mention that I was becoming overheated--not that I let myself be a victim to erratic weather? There, to my right, fifteen feet ahead of me like a beacon of safety, was a large parking spot waiting for me. Expertly I maneuvered the car into that spot in order to flee the heat and the chaos that seemed to be contaminating my reason.

That is when I noticed the sign for the "Happy Hour." Now for many of you not familiar with the seedier side of Minneapolis, the Happy Hour is what is called a gay bar. You may ask how I know. You see despite the irrefutable fact that my behavior is perfectly proper, I have a slight peccadillo, or should I say a slight, potential peccadillo. I am attracted to the less fair sex. Not that I go to bars or otherwise engage in a lifestyle that was and probably still should continue to be illegal in these United States. The law after all is supreme, simply ask the revered Hadrian.

Now, I had long ago rightly learned to hold all but the meager-est of desires at bey. After all, as a history professor, I had learned the disastrous price that otherwise sober men pay for pleasure, but I was feeling faint and the sidewalk seemed to tilt towards that door that promised cool darkness. It was the end of summer after all; one little visit would not hurt. Not that I normally notice endings. That kind of nostalgia, or for that matter any kind of nostalgia is bad form. Only fools allow themselves to be touched by something that has no name, the kind of sentimental fools that sit in bars in the afternoon.

It certainly was not carnal desire that impelled me towards that doorway into a darkness of forbidden mystery and rancid cigarette smoke. My ordeal of heat and noise seemed to be taking its toll on my otherwise finely honed constitution. I pushed through the door reeling, and for an instant imagined myself in some Roman god's smoky shrine, seeking some answer…and let me tell you, imagination has never been one of my defects. There in the center of the room behind what looked like an altar, stood a luminous young man with the knowing look of a high priest. He presided over an array of mysterious bottles, pouring libations into the glasses held by the shadowy supplicants standing around him in the darkness.

I steadied myself; the cool air was beginning to have its intended affect. That annoying sense of shadowy mystery began dissipating, and suddenly I was back in the tawdry bar. Despite my well earned reputation for good taste, I was relieved to recognize the ordinary vulgarity of that scene: no priest, no altar, no supplicants, only that tart of a bartender surrounded by middle aged men who should have had better things to do. Occasional pointless laughter punctuated the murmur of whispered, catty secrets. It was only then that I heard the pumping music.

"Sweet Dreams are made of these
(Eurythmics)

Who am I to disagree?
Some of them want to hurt you
Some of them want to be hurt by you.
Who am I to disagree?
Sweet dreams are made of these..."

My bearings and dignity once more secured, I began looking for an empty stool, some place a bit set apart but still close enough to observe that vulgar place. Just as I was rounding the bar, one of those dim faces turned in my direction staring straight at me.

"Why don't you sit down? I've been waiting for you."

He looked at me as if in recognition. His face was pale. It gleamed out of the shadow as if it had some inner source of illumination. His eyes burned like stars. I, Julian Scribner, actually looked away for a moment wondering if I were still under the influence of the beastly heat. Of course I quickly looked back, ready to stake out my territory and defend it if necessary. Assuming a more magisterial distance, I studied his face. Why, he looked like some night-blooming flower: tender, preposterous and passive. Dark hyacinth curls tumbled over his glowing forehead, and I could make out a slight trembling in his lower lip. Though I certainly did not want to reinforce any of his delusions, I felt paralyzed by an unexpected and unwanted flush of some kind of fugue state, some, dare I say, sense of yearning.

"Sweet dreams are made of these
Who am I to disagree?"

Needless to say I am more accustomed to asking questions than to answering them. Now I found myself speechless.

The apparition gestured with a kind of forlorn sweetness to the empty seat next to him. "You haven't changed a bit." Then he smiled at me, the way an adult looks at a dear but obtuse child.

Did I mention that normally I am the person to give directions? I riled for a moment, but his smile seemed so full of affection. Now my peers and students treat me with due deference, but seldom have I ever seen anyone's face light up at my approach. Perhaps I was still dizzy from the heat of the afternoon, but I felt a certain urgency to respond to him. If I did not immediately jump through the window of his invitation, it might disappear, and I would be left forever lost. Not that being lost is a state which I normally consider, but truth be told I did not want him to turn away. I said, "Yes," and took my seat.

He glanced back at his drink for an instant and then stared off into space with a dreamy look. Finally he roused himself and with childlike intensity grabbed his glass of brown liquid. I heard the ice cubes clink as he swished the liquid around and pressed the brim of the glass to his lips. I remember the clinking so clearly. Perhaps none of the ensuing story would have happened if it were not for that delicate little sound, or at least if I had not heard it.

Suddenly he seemed very relieved. "I thought you would never come. You know I can't swim."

At first I refused to respond to his impertinent, presumptive absurdity. I have standards to maintain after all. That is when I noticed how his full lips were, like dewy petals. I decided quite generously that just this once I would honor his impertinence with a response. "I do not normally make a practice of going to these bars especially during the afternoon."

Far from appreciating my generosity, he looked as if I

had just pricked that tender, pale face of his with something sharp.

Absurdly I wanted to touch his cheek and give it a little apologetic pat, although usually I try to keep apologies to a minimum...I make so few mistakes.

He simply continued to sit there radiating sadness and dare I say beauty? I know that this is a feeble justification for my ensuing remark, but perhaps I had not really recovered from the heat. "Did any one ever tell you how charming you are?"

He looked straight at me and with a relieved smile said, "Take me home."

I took charge. "What are you doing at a bar on a Monday afternoon?"

His face tightened as if he had been poked again, and then it softened. "Please?"

It was only when we stepped out into the light, that I noticed his pale skin was etched with a fine network of wrinkles especially around his eyes, and his coal black hair was clearly the product of artifice. He was dressed in a gold colored tee shirt and blue jeans that would have been more appropriate for a much younger man. Indeed if he were a flower, it would be yesterday's. As if in apology, he said, "My name's Antony. You can call me Tony."

CHAPTER 2

A plain large institutional clock on a neutral colored wall ticks with steady resolution. The hour hand reaches 3 pm then stops--silence. Agnes, sitting at a desk under the clock, turns her very red-haired head to glance at the clock and then returns with hard faced irritation to her crossword puzzle. A placard on her desk reads, "History Department."

Sabina, a plaid shirted, boyish, fresh faced woman, on the slippery slope of 35, races into the room. With her free hand she pushes her long unruly tresses away from her face and places a piece of paper into the wire basket on Agnes's desk. Two coppery spirals hanging from her ears continue to shake even after she stops at the desk. She stands there for a moment, a Midwestern version of a Cretan goddess, peeking over Agnes's shoulder.

Agnes looks up, demanding, "Another word for a story that isn't true but is real."

For an instant the plaid shirted goddess looks as bewildered as any college freshman.

Agnes humorously complains. "What good are you anyway?"

Sabina examines the crossword puzzle. "Four letters and

has an "h" at the end." She suddenly comes to life. "Myth, try myth." Looking very pleased with herself she studies the puzzle earnestly counting out the letters.

Agnes scribbles in the letters and demands, "Okay Einstein, explain!"

Sabina frowns trying to find the right words. Then she shifts into a pedagogical tone of voice. She lectures now, very seriously. "You see, take Jesus or Buddha or let us take Santa Claus." She smiles a little too complacently at Agnes. "This man in a red suite riding in the sky on a sleigh pulled by reindeers, year after year, and children keep asking for presents from him. Sometimes they even get them. Jung might call this an archetype." Emphatically she bends down toward Agnes. "It isn't true, but has a deep life of its own. It's real without being concretely true…you see?"

Agnes looks unimpressed. "Like when George says he loves me."

Sabina is now deep in thought. "Not exactly."

Agnes scowls. "What are you bothering me for? I have work to do."

Julian, dressed in his usual black no-nonsense suite stands in the doorway watching the two women, an air of controlling disapproval on his face, just short of a sneer. He commences to pull two sheets of paper out of his black leather brief case.

Both women uneasily glance in his direction.

Julian marches up to the desk. "I need copies of this by 7 am tomorrow morning." He is too self-importantly busy to even make eye contact.

Agnes mutters to Sabina, under her breath. "Who died and left him in charge?

Julian coolly deposits the papers on the desk.

Agnes ignores him.

His fingers tap insistently on the pile of papers.

Agnes glares at Julian. "A twelve letter word for being born again and again…."

Julian looks bewildered.

Sabina focuses on the crossword puzzle then smiles in satisfaction. "Try reincarnation, a fractal pattern repeating through time, similar and surprising…both, and with a life of its own. You may even learn something from it if you pay attention." She grins at Agnes.

"Who wants to learn anything? I want George,"

Julian's face is turning red and his lips, always thin, disappear into the slash of his mouth. He glances at the clock. He has nowhere else to look. "Isn't anybody going to fix that clock?!"

Sabina smiles in an attempt to defuse the situation. "You're such a charmer; time stands still around you."

Agnes cackles.

With stiff dignity intact, obliviously he walks out of the room.

Agnes smirks at the clock and grabs the phone; she dials. "Would you get someone over here to fix my clock? It's driving Julian crazy; not that he isn't crazy already.

CHAPTER 3

How unfair it was then that the very minor transgression of a wrong turn would have such far reaching impact. After all, the world is littered with people who are reckless and even worse, while I, Julian Scribner, who am virtually blameless, pay the price for other peoples' carelessness. That is why rules are so important; you can actually place the blame at the doorstep of the profligate. If someone as careful as I, do happen to be involved in a mishap, clearly, someone else is at fault.

After my portentous rendezvous with Tony, I fought valiantly to maintain the blessed routine of my schedule; on the surface my life seemed unchanged. As usual, I got up in the morning at 4am., did some army calisthenics (both aerobic and anaerobic are essential you know), had a bowl of skim milk and bran flakes (of course no sugar), ate one piece of fruit (an apple on Sunday, a peach on Monday, six grapes on Tuesday, a plum on Wednesday, an orange on Thursday, a banana on Friday and on Saturday a tangerine), and finally sat at my computer exploring yesterday's research into the ancient world. At 7am, I packed my lunch, alternating steamed vegetables with a plain green salad (I avoid fatty dressings), and with a very final snapping shut of my briefcase, set out for my office at the University where I would drink a single cup of organic, decaffeinated coffee before the parade of students pleading there various causes would begin. I ask the questions.

Everything WOULD have been perfectly correct, except for the presence of Tony. After his fateful installation in my home (really an invasion of the subjunctive voice… how I disdain the hypothetical or anything that indicates impermanence), just as I would snap my briefcase shut he would step out of the bedroom in a towel draped loosely around his waist, his hair all limp and overblown, hanging down his forehead like a bouquet of yesterday's tulips. He has a sense of theater my Tony. Casual and drowsy, he would walk into the bathroom, but just before closing the door he would release the towel, so that out of the corner of my eye, I could see the promise of night time; and after all Tony is of that age when a distant glimpse is to be preferred. Up close there is a smell to an aging body, yeasty, as if the decay of death were already getting a head start. Fortunately I keep my age at bay. Though many deluded people believe that they do not look their age, believe me, I actually do not.

At any rate that sudden flash of fantasy with which Tony would treat me each morning, fueled my day with an expectation of delight; although I would never interrupt my routine to actually look up. Even on Mondays, when he could have stayed in bed, he performed his usual parade. Tony is a hair dresser; they always have Mondays off.

We settled into life, he and I. He stopped his forays into the depths of the Happy Hour. I rearranged the old periodicals and newspapers lying in neat, categorized piles throughout the house (I can hardly believe that people simply throw these important documents away.…certainly an ominous sign for our culture) and placed them carefully in sequence in the spare bedroom and along the sides of the hallway upstairs. For his part, he took me out to a Greek restaurant every Saturday evening and regaled me with stories about his family who sound like a sorry lot indeed.

I learned to eat egg plant and olives.

He continued to touch up his hair and meticulously shave his body.

I never reminded him about his age.

He praised my stamina.

I ignored the absurdities of his logic (certainly if he were a student of mine I would be encouraging him to try one of the very adequate and less logic intensive technical schools where he could get some sort of a certificate for caning chairs or making jewelry).

He continued to entertain me with bed time antics.

We became a couple.

How wonderful is the cultivated mind! I nurtured an appreciation for Tony's decaying mentation, which after all I could envisage as an aging cheese or fermenting wine. There was a certain bouquet and piquancy to those stories of his that grew in idiot complexity over time. His conversation about his family was particularly lunatic. It took me months to realize that his family was only comprised of three other people, a brother, sister, and mother. He kept giving them different names. Over time I realized that there were three basic kinds of stories. Each one of these kinds of stories could be identified with a family member. Specific names were relatively unimportant. I could identify the family member by his or her sorry predicament. I needed my signature brilliance to break the code and find a strand of meaning in Tony's chatter .

All stories concerning foolish sexual dalliances are

about the sibling he calls Cleo, Charlene, Charlotta, or even Darryl. All stories concerning a self righteous vicious prig are about Jerome, Heironimus, Jose, or Judith. Tony would at various times call his mother all sorts of muddled faintly mythological names: Mary, Hera, Kuan Lin, Kali. She appears to be the most international of the preposterous group. Thank goodness marriage between members of the same sex is illegal. Those people could be my in-laws.

What could I expect from Tony when he sprang from a group of people who changed their names with each new situation. Of all the absurdities! As if this remarkable self that I have created is simply a shell to be thrown off and replaced. Of course Tony lives in a medium of inconsistencies and contradictions: a boy in a middle aged body; a pouting, soft face, atop a torso, heavy-chested. He submerges the most pointless concern in extravagant enthusiasm. All and all he seems rather unmoored in this universe of space and time.

Occasionally I would catch him staring off as if to some far point into the aetherium. At those moments his face would empty into a look both puzzled and sad. It was probably just a bout of indigestion, but I would invariably feel some inner compulsion to comfort him. Absurd, is it not? You see already, subtly, chaos was invading my world. Perhaps if I had noticed it back then, I could have stemmed the tide.

Mondays were the days that Tony devoted to his mysteries. I do not hazard to guess what those entailed. When I would return on those evenings, he would meet me at the door glistening and smelling of thyme and roses, his hair splendidly renewed; artificially black as a moonless night. He would greet me with the hushed portentous tones of a high priest guarding a profound ritual in which I was privileged to participate. "Why Julian, come in." His right hand would theatrically sweep me into the dining room to view the table laden with Greek delicacies: moussaka, spanakopita, stuffed grape leaves…always a surprise, waiting as fragrant as his flesh in which soon I would also partake, and yes, relish. His need to please seemed so urgent.

Though I scrupulously avoid sentimental reminiscences, I recall one Monday, like so many of the others, yet somehow it chafes my memory. That evening breathlessly and perhaps slightly more urgently than usual Tony whispered in my ear as I entered the house, "Oh Julian, how wonderful to see you. I DO have something special for you tonight!" He winked at me while those blooming lips of his parted in moist innocence. Then just before he ushered me into the fragrant inner sanctum, he glanced out of the still open door as if he were afraid that someone or something were following me…he can be such a foolish creature at times. What could threaten a life as steadfast as mine? Like a Roman stoic of old, I pride myself on a certain inviolable serenity.

Rightly so, I ignored his apprehension as some sort of confusion resulting from his frequent exposure to the chemicals used in the beauty trade. He shut the door behind me with quiet apprehension and then looked away in one of those out of focus trances of his. He stood there as if he were absolutely frozen. I could not even see him breathe. Even my sense of time, usually as orderly as a clock, seemed to falter. Dare I say, I lost track of time? Whether that episode lasted a few second or a few minutes, I do not know. Then suddenly his strange fugue state was dispelled. Tony woke with a startle and began immediately talking about the outrages of his shopping day.

"Julian, you won't believe what a day this has been. I stopped at Nick's, that Greek delicatessen on Lake and Lyndale and they were out of that special extra virgin olive oil that I love. How can anyone who calls himself Greek run out of my special extra virgin olive oil?"

After six months of living with Tony, I had learned to respond with appropriate horror. I knew that If I did not respond with enough sympatico to his emotional outbursts, he would become dreadfully concerned about my emotional well being and prod my privacy with hovering, care taking questions. He would finish those intrusions off with a bout of lip pouting disappointment. I've always hated to disappoint anyone who tries so hard.

Evidently I had indicated enough open mouthed horror this time, and he passed on to the next topic. "I stopped by that new coffee shop on 24th Street, the one everyone is talking about. It's been so terribly cold this winter, so much snow. What a tragedy to live in this horrible climate; why couldn't it be more like…"

I nodded benignly, not willing to take the time to wait for this train of thought. "It is only a fool who is at the mercy of the weather."

He did not seem comforted by my reassurance. In fact he appeared strangely ill at ease. "I decided to see what everybody was talking about, that new coffee shop…The Empire." He stared at me for a moment as if he were dropping a clue. Tony can be so full of the foolishly melodramatic.

He glanced at me with fluttery disingenuous confidentiality, almost like he was hiding something. "And Julian, when I stepped through that door, not wanting to make a scene, there right in front of me, almost like he was waiting for me, sat this person. The whole room seemed to spin around him…the center of the world, as if when he was around, nothing, nothing else mattered. I almost stumbled over him. He was so…I don't have words for it…I didn't know what to do"

He stared at me with bizarre urgency, begging for some kind of understanding. These old homosexuals are such drama queens, making something out of nothing.

I ignored him and sat down at the food-laden table, after all everything was as usual.

I nodded between bites of pastitsa. That topic was officially ended. I do not like my digestion to be disturbed.

But he kept up the nagging story. "You would know it, but the coffee house was reeking with cigarette smoke."

I nodded in deep sympathy, and did not ask him how he tolerated all those desperate and smoky afternoons in his old alma mater, The Happy Hour.

"I just hate the way that cigarette smell saturates my hair, especially after I have just worked on it." He patted his dark glistening curls and looked at me as if I were supposed to admire his artificially colored locks.

I knew I needed to say something soon. "Your hair looks lovely as usual my dear."

At first he looked extravagantly pleased; then his face once again startled, froze for just a second in something like terror or great anticipation. His words began speeding up. "I almost bumped into him. There I am standing six inches away. Just to be courteous, I told myself, so I gave him my name. He said that his name was Adrian. He stared at me for the longest time"

Tony stood there dumbly motionless. Then his foolishness evaporated and was replaced with that strange look, part sadness, part fear, part anticipation. Now normally I do not like to consider, let alone respond to what other people are feeling, but after all, in that moment, frozen in time, I had nothing else to do.

Then Tony snapped out of that strange altered state, back to his usual silliness. "Well, what can I expect after all?

I could see his green eyes pierce the smoke. I noticed that he had no shirt on, just a black leather vest as shiny as his sweaty, muscular arms, like some hero of old, like one of those old Italian muscle epics." Tony glanced at me apologetically. "Not that you aren't masculine in your own way."

I withheld any response. I hate to be patronized.

Tony, once again in his deluded excitement, did not notice. He fluttered on. "And I looked at his neck and thick shoulders, all warm and brown even in this horrid season. And he had golden hair all over his torso." He glanced at me apologetically (as if I were lacking something). "Not that I am not absolutely enthralled by your more austere chest."

Then he turned away from me. I hope in deep remorse. How dare he compare me to that obvious ruffian?

Tony's excitement once again began mounting in urgency, as if he were getting ready to jump off of a very high precipice. "Of course he's so young, and though I do my best to salvage the remnants of my beauty...he's so young after all. You know how I'm absolutely devoted to you Julian? I don't know what came over me." Tony peeked up at me, not just embarrassed as he certainly should be, but with desperate longing, as if he wanted something from me, even after his flagrantly insulting remarks.

I cleared my throat and gave him a well deserved look of bitter reproach. Enough is enough after all. "He sounds like rough trade to me my dear. It amazes me how people can be drawn to such cheap and obvious charms."

Tony's head cocked to the side as if he were considering some disturbing possibility. "Thank goodness Nick is expecting olive oil tomorrow."

CHAPTER 4

An early fall morning, the sun just beginning to illuminate the gray, Julian in his black suite marches into his drab kitchen. He frowns as he notices garlic and onions and tomatoes filling the surface of the plain wooden kitchen table. Turning away from the culinary chaos he scrutinizes his image in the small plain mirror above the sink. He straightens his tie which is already straight, smiling at himself with icy approval. He opens a cupboard and without looking, and takes a cup from line of cups on the shelf. He fills the cup with water from his filtered faucet and centers it in front of the blender. He opens the freezer compartment of the refrigerator, pulling out a clear plastic bag with brown curved objects inside. He pulls out one of those objects. Friday…it's a frozen banana. He centers it immediately behind the blender but at a right angle to a greenish container labeled POWDERED SEA KELP. Then he studies the tableau for a moment just to make sure that it is perfect.

Then with absolute confidence and without even looking he pours the cup of water into the blender, then adds exactly one scoop of powdered sea kelp. While admiring his water-filtration system he plops the brown and frozen banana into the green liquid and switches on the blender. An unappealing greenish frothy mixture forms in the belly of the blender. He pours the green liquid back into the cup with automatic confidence. He whispers to himself, "I keep my diet pure and my life correct."

Suddenly he looks up, startled, and then annoyed. The sound of footsteps creak down the old wooden stairs in the living room. He quickly pours the frothy green mess down his throat. With one big gulp he swallows the liquid.

Tony appears at the doorway of the kitchen, a towel around his waist, an amulet hanging from a chain around his neck. The morning sun glints on the golden bird, resting on his naked chest. With both hands he lifts the chain over his head.

Julian places the glass down by the sink. Unfortunately he is wearing a gob of green froth on his upper lip.

Tony spots it and smiles. "Just like a naughty little boy."

Julian looks outraged.

Tony watches the transformation with tender sadness. He delicately walks over to Julian, and with an end of his towel, Tony wipes the green goo off Julian's lip.

Julian stares aghast at the green smudge on the towel.

Tony with a strange little smile on his face gives the chain and amulet to Julian. "We all need a second chance."

Julian, too shaken by the encounter, allows Tony to place the chain over his head. Julian stares at the offending amulet now hanging from his neck. "What is THAT for? You should know that I do not go in for such foolishness!" He pulls it off with disgust, waving his hand, amulet dangling from it. "Enough of this foolishness!" His expression softens slightly. "At the least I approve of your conscientious hygiene."

Tony turns toward the bathroom, dropping his towel.

Julian watches Tony's naked back and almost smiles. Absentmindedly he picks up his briefcase and stuffs the amulet inside it. He has important things to do.

CHAPTER 5

Julian's dark figure steps down the cement steps of the pillared History Building, the end of a glorious spring afternoon. He is totally oblivious to the students frolicking on the grass.

Julian mutters quietly, "Sabina, Sabina, Sabina. When will you ever learn?"

At that very instant. A huge, shirtless body slams into him, knocking him off his feet. The contents of his briefcase spill across the grass. Julian lies, dazed. Finally he looks up at the huge figure standing above him, set against the blue sky.

The apparition mutters. "Football…" He waves the pigskin at Julian.

Julian shakily sits up.

The student bends down and picks up something glistening in the grass, the amulet of the bird. At first he looks at it casually, then something catches his attention. His whole bleary focus condenses on that one shiny object. He mutters automatically as if in a trance, "Yes, yes, finally." He forces his attention away from that gleaming bird and begins studying Julian as if looking for something, or perhaps even trying to remember.

Getting his bearings, Julian's shattered dignity begins to coalesce. He fixes his eyes on the offending student. "What beastly foolishness!" Julian's face turns fiercely contemptuous. "How many times do I have to tell students that they have to maintain SOME kind of decorum on campus?" He staggers to his feet, studying the student's face now. "Aren't you the brute that shouldered me off the road two weeks ago?" This is more an accusation than a question. He presses his point disdainfully. "You drive that vulgar purple Imperial convertible."

The Adrian ignores Julian and ever so gently places the golden bird into his jeans pocket.

For a moment Julian watches, strangely silent and submissive.

Adrian turns away.

The docile moment is past; Julian brushes his pants off. "The very least you could do is introduce yourself. Has not anyone taught you manners?"

The young man starts walking away speaking with clear authority now. "Adrian."

At a loss for words Julian watches the figure disappear into the bright day. With as much decorum as possible he begins putting his belongings, strewn across the grass, back into his brief case. Finally he once again stiffly sets off across the campus commons.

Julian picks his way through the row upon row of cars in the campus parking lot as if they were beneath his notice. Finally he approaches his impeccably clean old BMW. He smiles at it with approval and reaches into his briefcase, his hand searching the contents. He begins to look bewildered; pulling the briefcase open he examines the contents more carefully…nothing. For an instant he looks like a forlorn child.

Just then a large lumbering pudding-faced person of indeterminate gender also enters the parking lot. The way she/he moves, the way she/he dresses, the person seems caught in some kind of borderline zone between the genders. The person notices Julian's distress and walks toward him rapidly. In a tentative, apologetic high pitched voice the person asks, "Can I help you?"

Julian stiffens and says sarcastically, "You think you can do something, do something for me?" He looks outraged.

The person looks down, embarrassed.

"Bobbie, or whatever silly name you want to be called now, what makes you think that I have any kind of problem? Is it illegal to look inside my briefcase?"

Bobbie shakes his head sadly and walks away apostrophizing in a strangely deep voice, "Life's but a shadow…a tale told by an idiot, full of sound and fury."

Julian starts laughing with muted hysteria. "The wise man always has a second set of keys." He reaches into the inside pocket of his black suite and pulls out a key. He looks toward Bobbie's disappearing form with righteous indignation.

CHAPTER 6

A darkened room, only slits of light glow at the edges of the blinds. The flashing computer screen illuminates Adrian's face. As his fingers frantically press the keys, images of Rome shine. Pictures of ancient sites, one after another fill the screen. Finally one picture reveals the Pantheon. He stares at it first in shock and then with recognition.

Underneath him the muffled sounds of young men joking and rough-housing disturb his concentration. He shakes his head in irritation and types in "HADRIAN." Pages of references pop up. His glowing face grins in wild excitement.

The door to the room opens and ordinary light shines on Adrian and into the very ordinary frat house bedroom. A good natured looking young man, holding a football in his hand, pants at the door as playful as a puppy. "How bout a game?" He tosses the ball into his other hand, looking at Adrian expectantly.

Adrian, ferociously absorbed by the computer screen ignores him.

For a moment the young man looks hurt. Then he

smiles, tossing the foot ball at Adrian. "Catch!" It hits the chair.

Slowly, as if under water Adrian turns toward the frat boy and stares. There is utter silence; even the sounds downstairs disappear.

Frat Boy's teasing smile evaporates.

Adrian holds his gaze.

Frat Boy looks down.

Adrian smiles coolly.

Frat boy glances up submissively. "I'll tell the guys to keep it down."

Adrian nods majestically.

CHAPTER 7

I shared my bed with Tony and my office with Sabina. This history (this is not a story after all; stories are contaminated with whimsy) unfortunately would not make sense without her. Years ago she had been one of my dear graduate assistants. Later I had to share my office with her; after all I am famous for my generosity. Though I did not consider her my peer, I accepted her as a junior colleague. I remember her very first visit to my office when she was a mere nubbins of undergraduate student. She was fresh from some absurd little town, Waseca, or Wadena, or perhaps Owatonna, some bit of pasture hardly deserving a name. She still smelled of corn and alfalfa.

I remember her first visit to my office, she was all out of breath; perhaps the poor dear had just come in from milking cows. "Are you professor Julian Scribner?"

I wondered who else she thought would have been sitting at my office, at my desk. I nodded magisterially. "And who have I the pleasure of addressing?" (I do not answer questions.)

She looked baffled for a moment, but finally gathering

her courage. She planted her two little feet apart and stared at me. "My name is Sabina, that's a Latin name!"

I smiled at her. "How lovely that people out in the country (notice the way I was too tactful to use the word 'peasant') pass those fine old names along, even if they mispronounce them."

Her head bowed in confusion.

I went on with my lesson. "You my dear pronounced it with a long "i". By rights if you were to pronounce it in proper Latin, it would be "Sabena"; the "i" is pronounced as a long "e". Now say it after me, this time correctly, "Sabena."

Her wispy, corn silk hair shook as if there had been a sudden gust of wind. Nevertheless, she repeated the proper pronunciation of her name. After all students need to learn a certain docility if knowledge is to be inseminated in them. Besides for the poor girl's sake I needed to instill in her an appreciation for hierarchy. I ignored the way that her lips pressed together while her cheeks blew out like a prickly blow fish.

Then with a totally inappropriate hauteur, she said, "Well Julian Scribner, YOU are my new advisor." She held her pencil out, pointing it at me as if it were some kind of a scepter; and I, her humble servant.

I gave her my stoniest stare and with simple dignity said, "We will see about that!." Despite the fact that I had certainly set her straight, I must admit that there was something charming about her, a kind of Joan of Arc pluck; although I would certainly need to stock up on matches. As far as her imperial airs, I would not even dignify them with a reaction. To tell the truth (which I always do), despite her rather uncouth tendencies, Sabina and I got on quite famously. She became my earnest protégé. Although back then I would have been shocked to know that I would eventually have to share an office with her. Fortunately for her, I never cling to grievances.

Despite her, shall we say unlettered background, she grew and ripened in the field of academia. Of course she had my almost constant support. She too, devoted herself to the study of ancient history, so great was her admiration for me. Somewhere late in her senior year, after I had already written her an eloquent letter of recommendation for graduate school here, she began becoming unhinged: she developed an interest in mythology. If I had known that this would be the disastrous result of all my sober instruction, I would have recommended that she go back to her roots and switch to the horticulture department. Perhaps there her hands would be kept so busy that her mind would not be addled by stories of randy gods and goddesses.

I remember the moment when I first realized that despite my best efforts, she was beginning to mount a subversive attack on the foundations of law. I was brilliantly elucidating some finer point of the *Justinian Digest*, that remarkable body of Byzantine law, which owed so much to Hadrian's *Edict Perpetuum*. The Byzantine emperor, Justinian, took that splendid edict of Hadrian's and solidified it even further. After all you can never make something too solid and strict. Justinian clarified the true eternal meaning of that edict so that it would be more appropriate for his later era, an era which was set into motion by that most sober of emperors, Constantine. He had the vision to align Roman law to the fast rising belief in the Christ. Brilliantly Constantine enhanced slightly fraying Roman authoritarianism (*authoritarianism*, I do not know why people are so afraid of that word) by making Christianity the state religion. He set in motion the destruction of all those messy little gods and goddesses, tearing down their temples and crushing their fanciful statues. All that crushed limestone was burned into lime. What a beautiful sight that must have been, to see all those idiot stories turned into calcium oxide. Now, just as all divine power had its source in the single Christian God, so all earthly power emanated from the single earthly ruler, but I will not get into the significance of that right now.

CHAPTER 8

Bobbie, a toga hanging on her bulky body, nervously steps up to the open mike. Her foot catches on a chair in front of the stage. Her whole body convulses in embarrassment as she let's out a high pitched, "OOOOPS!"

A few faces look up and then turn back to their conversations at the Empire. These patrons are a varied group, younger grunge kids, then some suburban kids trying to look grunge, then older people, leftovers from the sixties trying to find place to land, and finally solitary people hunched over computers or talking with anonymous people on cell phones; everyone casually ignoring Bobbie.

Sabina always game for costuming, sits at a table near the front of the audience dressed in the facsimile of a roman woman's tunic.

Once Bobbie finally stumbles up to the microphone, he looks to Sabina for reassurance.

She nods in ferocious support.

There is a strange pause, a kind of blank in the progression of time, the door of the Empire opens and Adrian steps into the room, dressed in a leather vest, surveying his realm.

Everyone except Bobbie and Sabina stare at him.

Bobbie glances once more at Sabina, and then adopts a heroic posture. She begins to recite the Aeneid in deep, masculine voice. The Latin words resound through the room.

Without asking, Adrian sits in the chair next to Sabina. "I've been looking for you."

With irritation she turns toward the stranger. Startled, she tries to avoid eye contact with him.

Bobbie, ever-protective, notices. She frowns and stumbles over a Latin phrase.

Adrian nods imperially to Bobbie. "Splendid, do go on."

And Bobbie does.

Adrian again fixes his attention on Sabina. "It's been ages."

Her eyes are drawn to Adrian's gaze.

He nods ever so slightly, reaching into his vest pocket. He pulls out the golden bird.

Sabina watches him mesmerized.

He dangles it in front of her.

She reaches toward Adrian and the phoenix-bird.

Like in a game, he moves it ever so slightly out of her reach.

Bobbie watches helplessly.

Adrian clasps the bird in his hand, smiling ferociously.

CHAPTER 9

B ut to get back to Sabina; I had been cautioning her
about the inappropriateness of her interest in mythology.
Instead of facing me humbly with her head slightly bowed,
she was staring out the window. Suddenly she said, 'I'm
crazy about crows.'

I judiciously ignored the inappropriate comment, and
reiterated how Roman law from Augustus to Hadrian to
Justinian demonstrated the evolving simplification that
serves as a sober foundation for western thought and religion.

She glanced at me with a baffled look on her face, not
with assenting gratitude, but in utter amazement. I try not
to amaze people; it is too messy.

She said, "I wonder if Hadrian would have been pleased
that Constantine's unholy marriage of church to state would
eventually demote his boyfriend Antinous from divine to
mortal status?"

I studied her face for a moment; it had a kind of loose but
intense look as if she were taking in my precious knowledge
and then actually and unwisely thinking on her own. I
responded with my most forgiving tone of voice, a very
definite and pointed tone that indicated the gravity of her

betrayal. "My dear, do you not see that all the emperors set themselves up as gods and anyone else who struck there fancy? In spite of Hadrian's unquestioned brilliance he had this little altogether insignificant peccadillo. He is said to have appreciated the beauty of boys. When you grow up my dear you will understand that even the most absolutely upright of us may have some minor folly that certainly does not diminish the sterling rectitude of our lives."

Sabina though appropriately silent, did not look altogether convinced. She shook her corn silk hair, widened her stance and stared at me with tight lips and bulging blow fish cheeks.

Far from becoming a true historian, I could see that Sabina was becoming a gossip monger, so like her sex.

She blew out the air captured in her cheeks, and I could tell that her lips were beginning to form the word, "but."

Very gently I made one last attempt to set her straight. "Sabina! After all the effort I have taken with you, I am disappointed to see that your scholarship is so misguided. If you had a true appreciation for the Roman world, you would realize that those gods were nothing more than a source of entertainment for the Romans, a diversion from bridge building. Even the almost faultless Hadrian needed some kind of occasional break. I should not have to remind you that Hadrian knew that only laws provide true meaning to life. Only the law is immortal, not some silly boy from Bithynia. I hope that this is not an indication of the kind of graduate student you are destined to become!"

She looked absent-mindedly out the window and repeated, "Yes, the crows are beginning to come right into the city. There was a time when they stayed in the country. Funny, isn't it?"

But funny it was not. She was clearly slipping into a morass of fuzzy defiance. As if the door of her mind, which I had so graciously helped shut against the onslaught of irrationality, were opening, leaving a gaping hole in the edifice of her education; leaving her vulnerable to deplorable, wistful fantasy. All too clearly, that door and her mind were becoming unhinged. I pleaded with her to just say no to the forces of chaos that hide under the seductive guise of wishful, romantic thinking.

Besides, she did not and still does not have the proper looks for romance; it just does not suite short people. Her features serve as a virtual catalogue for the prosaic. She has a solid body; and not that I really notice, small breasts. Her bangs already beginning to gray, hung like a listless fringe above her dark glasses. She preferred to wear no nonsense slacks, plaid shirts, and shoes that only a nurse could love. Our Sabina just did not have the figure for fantasy.

For the sake of her own well being, I made one last attempt to prod her back into the corral of intellectual propriety. "Think girl! Stop right now before it is too late! I know what I am talking about. Unless you get a hold of yourself, you will loose any shred of academic sobriety that I have managed to instill in you."

Like some foolish billows, her cheeks puffed out again. She jerked her head back in my direction. Her stocky body coiled in unseemly antagonism. I do not know what came over the poor girl; it was certainly nothing that I said. Finally those defiant cheeks of her deflated with a kind of hissing sound. She stared straight at me. "Your righteous Hadrian! After the death of his paramour, Antinous, he spent the last eight years of life moaning around and making stupid decisions and losing so much power that finally he couldn't even get anyone to put him out of his misery. You call that sobriety? At least the gods weren't prigs."

I did not realize that the poor girl had such an unbalanced

animosity toward Hadrian. Her irrational hostility certainly could not have been directed at me. I have always been so helpful to her. Perhaps she was in the midst of one of those messy, female monthly binges. You know, that bloody tide which controls women's mood. How grateful I am to be a male and in control of the whimsies of nature! Or perhaps she was just paying the price for her interest in those unbalanced, flighty pagan deities. I knew then that she deserved pity. With great dignity I simply said, "If you are going to be that way about it, see if I care."

I knew then and there that she was lost to the study of Roman law. Previously I had entertained the possibility that someday she might be a successor to my endeavors, but she was lost, truly lost. Fair man that I am and a man of my word, I still occasionally pass on choice words of wisdom to her.

In her ensuing years of graduate school, she wallowed in myth, preferring the company of those goddesses and gods that were the plague of the ancient world. She let her hair grow out and began dressing differently: fancy shawls from India, Chinese silk, jewelry from Guatemala, she even set a small pot bellied statue of some primitive goddess on her desk. At times, if I must say so myself, Sabina looked all together demented. The rest of the department seemed to coddle her; I alone understood the gravity of her betrayal.

After receiving her doctorate, she actually interviewed for a position here. As usual, I was a good sport and except for occasional appropriately corrective remarks, I did not actively work against her being hired.

After she joined our ranks (much against my better judgment), I suffered my sense of moral outrage with quiet dignity. But really how could that fuzzy thinking girl have been invited into the rational heights of professional academia? Fortunately I was a full professor and could at least do my utmost to prevent her from rising to that august status. To increase my travail, the head of our department, that sniveling dean of the department, Peder Faucus, (He loves to correct peoples' pronunciation of his first name. "My name is 'Peder' not Peter;" anything to enable him to establish a false sense of superiority) actually moved her into my office. If I did not know how much he and all my peers, for that matter, hold me in the highest esteem, I would have thought it was a calculated insult. I finally realized that she was placed next to me so that I could continue to mentor her; I am famous for my mentoring skills.

Despite his betrayal of me, I maintained a dignified relationship with Peder; I did tell him though that if he did not have some kind of partition set up (I get the window) he would be sorry. Fortunately Peder is a coward (he would not even be the dean of the department if his uncle weren't on the board of regents), and the partition was scheduled to be erected the following day. I brought in coffee and donuts very early that next morning to give to those dear plebian construction workers; I made sure that the partition was moved a few inches to the right, so that my office would be a little bigger than Sabina's. Someone in this department needs to maintain standards.

Her office now is a thin partition from mine, and though I have finally stopped offering my pearls to her grunting, hostile self (notice the way I was too much of a gentleman to call her a swine), I could not help but notice her outlandish appearance and all her ridiculous paraphernalia.

I finally resigned myself to living next to that sentimental chaos. I know that for any really thoughtful student, she, Sabina, would serve as an abject reminder of what can happen if sober caution is thrown to the wind. I continue to be polite to Sabina. In fact when I would pass her in the hallway I give her a little smile of sympathy.

CHAPTER 10

The late afternoon light of August glows through the window revealing a large institutional bathroom, drab floors, pale tiles; everything is a cold shade of gray. From one of the closed stalls, the sound of flushing echoes through the bathroom. A somber looking Julian steps out. The campus bell tolls three times. He looks at his watch and frowns. Peeved, he walks over to the sink, once again uneasily looking at his watch. He straightens his already straight tie. For just an instant he stares into space, his face almost vulnerable.

A ferret-faced little man scurries into the bathroom. He glances around slyly as if he were scoping out his lair. He notices Julian, lost in thought. The ferret faced man smiles maliciously and clears his throat.

Julian startles than quickly assumes a haughty expression. Icily he says, "Peder, how nice to see you. Is this where you are accustomed to spend your time?" Julian stairs at Peder through the mirror.

For an instant Peder looks guiltily at that image in the mirror, and smiles back conspiratorially. "You look like you've seen a ghost."

Julian looks confused for a moment, then turns away from the mirror to stare down Peder. "How utterly absurd!"

Peder looks down slyly.

Julian watches with satisfaction. "I wish someone would see to it that those bells actually rang on the hour." He impatiently taps his finger on the face of his wrist watch. "If I were in charge…"

Peder looks up slyly. "What time do YOU have?"

Julian confidently looks at his watch, "4:45, exactly."

"Why Julian, I think." He smiles with great relish, "You're wrong."

Julian looks confused for an instant then recovers. "It's this watch. I am punctual." He studies Peder's slovenly appearance. "After all we are role models for our students. " He struts out of the room clutching his briefcase.

He marches out of the pillared building into the cloudy dimming light.

Three young men are watching his departure from a distance. One of them, Adrian, gestures and the rest follow him, heading toward the pillared history building. Adrian posts one young man at the foot of the stairs, and the other two follow him into the building.

Everything is quiet, lifeless in Julian and Sabina's office. The sound of someone fiddling with the lock jars the stillness. The door opens. Adrian steps in quietly, motioning to a young man posted in the hallway. Adrian closes the door behind him and studies both offices carefully.

First he looks at Sabina's area: goddesses, masks and fabrics. He studies a plaque with her name on it. His strong hands pick up a picture of Sabina and Bobbie; he smiles coldly.

He goes over to Julian's office and methodically opens

and searches the drawers. He finds an empty envelope with Julian's address on it and puts it in his pocket.

He notices a bust in the corner and walks over to it, a Roman head: "Hadrian the Magnificent." He stares at it intensely. His hands gently stroke his own face. Through the window, the last light of the afternoon breaks through the clouds and shines on the bust.

CHAPTER 11

As usual I continued to rise above the common, messy lot of most humans. My life moved in its usual, but brilliant course, even with the minor delicious inconvenience of Tony; after all he really was not supposed to interfere with my life. At least so it seemed until Christmas came that year. Every Christmas I pay my allegiance to the Roman liturgy with its Christian deity of law. Pope John Paul is as close to a hero as I have. Although I do think that if it were I under that triple tiara, things would run even more smoothly. I go to St. Mary's Catholic Basilica for high mass on Christmas Eve to celebrate the anniversary of that marriage of the bride of Christ to the commanding groom of Roman law. What a fortunate event! As the Roman world reached it's zenith at the time of Hadrian and then began to slowly fade, Christianity, the hand maiden, was there in the wings ready to pick up those cool, crisp absolute laws. Indeed on Christmas day I celebrate the reincarnation of the immortal judge.

Normally I do not make public appearances with Tony. He is after all my little lapse, but that Christmas I made an exception, or rather was cornered into making an exception. After I had shaved, donned my black suite, and was just about to leave, Tony peeked his tussled, dyed head out of the bedroom door. "Going to work on Christmas Eve, honey?" Then he pouted at me.

For a moment I, Julian Scribner, felt a pang of something like guilt…how absurd! I should have stopped right in my tracks, taken two aspirin and gone to bed. Surely guilt is an indication of a very momentary psychological imbalance, but instead, perhaps unduly influenced by the contaminating sentiment of the season, I slackened my vigilance. "Tony, I am just going to the Basilica, you would not want to come."

His head tilted to the side and his eyes opened into wide pools of sorrow. I could not stand it. I could not stand to see him sad; it is so messy. "I guess it will not hurt anything if you come along, but hurry up or I will be late. You know how I hate to be late."

He looked at me like a child saved from a terrible fate, and to be fair to him, he did get ready a little more speedily than usual. We were five minutes late; the priest decked out in all his ancient Roman attire was already parading into the sanctuary. As we stepped further into that cavern of the basilica filled with straining organ notes and smoky incense, I carefully and uncomplainingly explained to Tony that normally I would sit up front to drink in the spectacle, but because of him we would have to squeeze into one of the unseemly back pews.

He nodded, too excited to be apologetic.

I led the way into a shadowy pew. Just as I was settling into a fine state of decorum, who should walk in as if we were all waiting for her…Sabina. Now forgiving as I am, I would have liked to give her credit for dressing appropriately for that solemn event. Unfortunately I over estimated her sense of decorum. She walked in, 10minutes late, with a black lace mantilla draped over her not altogether clean tresses of hair, but underneath that facade of propriety, she was accoutered in a very tight, short, pink dress, leaving exposed vast expanses of pudgy leg barely covered in black fishnet stockings. In fact as I looked closer I realized that the lace pattern of her decorous mantilla matched the pattern of those scandalous stockings. What a terrible insult to those sober proceedings! It was too much for any man to stand. As she sauntered into the very same pew which I inhabited, I cast a silent, reproving look at her. I wanted everyone else in the basilica to understand that I, Julian Scribner, was definitely not connected to this blasphemy in fish net. The world would also know that I was too large a person to verbally acknowledge her presence. I was just beginning to feel comfortable in my indignation when I heard little whisperings going on to my left, from the direction of Tony and Sabina. There they knelt uttering little, annoying intimacies to each other instead of commemorating this solemn anniversary.

"Are you with him?" Sabina motioned at me as if I were the one creating a scene.

"Yeh, do you know him?"

"Yeh, my name's Sabina. We teach in the same department."

"Nice to meet you Sabina. My Name's Tony. I live with him."

"You don't say..." She glanced at me with malicious satisfaction.

I discretely kicked Tony under the pew.

Again I heard a whisper to my left. "Oops, I guess I better not whisper so loud, but it's really nice meeting you Sabina. Maybe we can talk after this is all over, since we're both friends of Julian. I never get to meet his friends."

"You're on, Tony."

Mercifully the annoying chit chat stopped long enough for the Mass to continue. Although I must admit that the proceedings were a bit baroque for my taste. Though I faithfully honor this reincarnation of the Divine Law, I regret the fact that Catholicism has kept so much of the mythological mess, those mystery cults of Rome and Greece where people became ecstatic and ate each other, all in the promise of some personal salvation. Even Hadrian that wise ruler and law maker toyed with the Elysian Revels. Of course, as I said before, that was simply entertainment for him, an interlude between constructing aqueducts.

While "Adeste Fideles" pounded out of the organ and the choir sang a rendition of that hymn in vulgar English (What a tragedy that Latin is no longer used!), Tony and I made our exit. Unfortunately I was forced right into the arms of a difficult situation that demanded, shall we say, delicate explanations.

Once we stepped out of the door of the basilica, Sabina who had followed us with her fuzzy innuendo, moved in for the kill.

"Why Julian how delightful to meet your companion. He is your companion isn't he?"

"My dear this is the last place I expected to see you, the celebration of the birth of the triumphant, rational male."

"Triumphant male? Why I was celebrating the anniversary of the Great Mother opening her legs and birthing another god." Sabina actually paused on the basilica steps and spreading her legs, and started singing "Remember the Red River Valley."

I tried to shield a young child passing by from this undignified and lewd attempt at humor; as if anything that sprang from between a woman's legs had a place near this enlightened building. After all, since Catholics believe that Mary remained a virgin even after conception and giving birth, Christ must have sprung out from some more dignified orifice.

Tony looked thrilled with his new, grotesque little friend. "Sabina why don't you drop over for a drink, I'd love to get to know one of Julian's friends. Doesn't he look sweet and solemn, so much like a little altar boy? I want to know all about you too, girl to girl"

She smiled at him conspiratorially, "I'll tell you about my new boyfriend; he's a real hunk, kind of mythic."

Politely I tried to put a stop to this familiarity. "Tony haven't you made enough of a scene already tonight? Besides we have an early morning tomorrow, and you certainly need your beauty sleep."

His head tilted to the side pouting, and his lower lip stuck out so far that a helicopter could have landed on it.

This time I did not relent. This catastrophe on the basilica steps was the result of my attempt at kindness. It was the price I pay for my sweet nature!

But Sabina had already found the chink in my armor. "Tony I'd love to come over sometime and see where you two live. You two do live together don't you?"

"You'll come over then sometime?" Tony had retracted his lower lip.

"I wouldn't miss it for the world. Why Julian you never told me that you have a significant other. Imagine that."

"He's quite insignificant, my dear, I can assure you."

Unfortunately Tony and Sabina got along famously, you know, birds of a feather flock together. Over the next few months, Tony taught Sabina how to make moussaka and babaganoosh, and I hesitate to think what she was teaching him, except that now when I lectured him on some fine point of Roman law over our spanakopita, I thought I could detect just a soupcon of insolence.

Finally to put a stop to this insurrection, I instructed Tony not to invite Sabina over or to talk with her on my phone. After all I am pater familias; this is my house, and a man's house is his castle. That should have put a halt to their unfortunate alliance. He pouted at first, but gently and firmly (years ago I had taken a course in dog training; I thought it would help with my students), I told him that the consequence of his disobedience would be banishment to the squalid life out of which I had plucked him. I am nothing if not fair.

It seemed though, that almost every time I entered my house now and stepped into the kitchen, Tony would bow his puffy face to avoid eye contact with me, and then with embarrassed submissiveness, grin, nestling close against me. I truly detest subterfuge. As he squirmed against me I would freeze, and then very casually say, "Have you been on the phone, my dear?" Then I would smile at him reproachfully. Not that I would actually accuse him of outright betrayal since I did not have absolute proof. Did I mention that I am always fair? I could have stooped to spying on him from outside the window, but this would be beneath my dignity. Besides there was a very large icicle hanging from the roof above the kitchen window. My life is too valuable to the world to risk impalement.

Despite my most valiant efforts that gradual erosion of my most excellent world was running its course. I, Julian Scribner, was having trouble with time, actually with clocks to be more precise. First my ever faithful Swiss watch began randomly stopping and starting. Of course I brought it to a jeweler who took two weeks to tell me that he could find nothing wrong with it. He had the gall to suggest that I had been forgetting to wind it. Indeed all the clocks around me seemed to becoming erratic. Tony, who was caught in his own particular time warp, hardly noticed. Even my office clock kept betraying me. People stopping by my office would ask me what time zone I was in. How dreadfully embarrassing! I who had virtually served as a measure of exactitude for those around me, had to actually ask for the time of day from perfect strangers. Standards, what was happening to my standards? Once during my freshman symposium on the last of the Roman emperors (let me tell you a sorry lot, certainly a let down from Hadrian) the clock on the wall must have stopped. I had long since given up the use of my watch. I was caught in flagrante, so excited in the details of Roman history that I had lost track of time; I had to ask my students for my temporal bearing. By some accident they gave me the wrong time and I let class out thirty minutes early. I am absolutely sure that this was an accident since all my students certainly appreciate the elaborate yet lucid details of my lectures. I did though assign them an extra ten page paper.

I cannot unfortunately give the benefit of my graciousness to sniveling Peder. He is reigning dean of the department. My colleagues have never asked me to be chairman. I am certain that this is not a slight. They simply do not want to waste my invaluable skills on petty bureaucratic tasks. But to get back to Peder, the whole department was to have a very important meeting that day in which I could once again demonstrate my fine critical mind…I noticed that my office clock had stopped again. Just then Peder stuck his head in my doorway, not a pleasant sight. His extravagantly curled red eye brows form an uninterrupted line over his calculating, squinty eyes. These far from appealing features are set in a face with the unpleasant, moist pallor of so many red-haired people. I wish he could keep his chin pointed downward. He is always craning his neck up, and I am forced to witness the spectacle of his Adam's apple jerking up and down his scrawny neck.

Besides, he spends entirely too much time sticking his fingers in the various orifices of his face; his nostrils seem to be his particular favorite targets. If he were not the nephew of a very important member of the board of regents, I am sure that he would be where he truly belongs, frying hamburgers at a fast food restaurant and wiping his roaming fingers on unsuspecting sesame buns.

Fortunately I am a tolerant man. I asked Peder for the time.

"Why Julian, it's 2P.M.; you have an hour before the meeting. We are all so interested in hearing your latest exposition."

Of all the disloyal perfidy! Peder lied to me. I arrived at the meeting at what I thought was the appropriate time only to find that I was an hour late. My fellow department members were already leaving. Without my cogent criticisms, that convocation was ending shamefully early. As for Peder… slings and arrows of vulgar men and women affect me not. I did though anonymously send him a box of rubber gloves with the note, "For the sake of hygiene, you might want to wear these during your excavations."

My life continued on its serene course until early March. Since having an office next to Sabina, I always regrettably knew when her primitive anniversaries occurred. She always accelerated her bizarre behavior in anticipation of those unsavory events. She drapes the fat little goddess on her desk with flowers and begins humming more loudly than usual those mournful, middle eastern melodies of which those bulbous deities must be fond; I found an invitation casually lying on my very neat desk.

> "Come join me on March 21 to express gratitude to the Goddess Demeter who once again has rescued her daughter, Persephone, from the grip of Hades, thereby ushering in spring.
>
> Sabina
> B.Y.O.R."

Underneath that, in her usual messy handwriting was scribbled, "Julian, the whole department would love to meet your Tony."

That she would dare contaminate me with her mythological offal! There was even a typo in that pathetic invitation. Though I am definitely NOT on the party circuit, even I know it is "B.Y.O.B.," or as fraternity boys (never a great source of subtlety), say "Bring Your Own Bottle."

As far as the implications of that ghastly post script… why the less said, the better.

I took that indictment of shoddy taste and immediately marched over to Sabina's side of the partition. She was sitting in her den of iniquity. "My dear, thank you for the delightful invitation. It is not often that I have received such a missive as this. I really hate to correct you thoigh, but do not you mean B.Y.O.B?"

She looked up from the chaos on her desk. "Why Julian, how kind of you to attempt to correct me again. I know how hard that must be for you." Her face melted into duplicitous sympathy. "But Julian, I do mean B.Y.O.R. Bring Your Own Ritual. Tony has told me how creative you are in the privacy of your bedfoom; come share some of your ingenuity with us. Surprise us."

Now I hate to be wrong; there is something so common and messy about it. After all I have a reputation for being right…always. "Well I regret to say, my dear, that I will have to deprive you and the whole department of my ingenuity. I have a previous, more important obligation."

She looked straight at me with deep concern. "Why Julian, you must be mistaken again. I just spoke with Tony this morning. He said that you never do anything at night. Perhaps you're simply suffering from a wee tad of memory loss. We all know how advanced you are in age. Next time I'm at the food coop I'll pick up some gingko tea for you. It does wonders for those flagging brain cells."

I froze into my most benign expression. Not only was she accusing me of being wrong, but the subtext of her remarks more than implied that I, Julian Scribner, was slipping into the advanced stages of senility. Why, with my careful diet, my scrupulously followed exercise regimen, and my so upright life, I will still be brilliantly teaching my courses while she is peeing down her leg in some nursing home. "How kind of you, Sabina, to consider my well being. Poor Tony, he can be so flighty sometimes. He must have forgotten that I have a MENSA meeting that night. You do know that I belong to MENSA, do you not? Your gracious invitation is so over powering though, that I suppose, just this once I can miss it."

Covering my tracks, decorously I began my exit.

Sabina smiled innocently. "Tony was so excited to hear that he was invited, and I know everyone in the office is dying to meet him."

Fair man that I am, on the way home I began imagining punishments that would appropriately match the severity of Tony's transgression. Yes, disembowelment was just a little bit too severe. As I entered the front door of my house, once again I thought I saw Tony slip his phone into his pocket. Did I mention that I hate subterfuge? I took a long slow look at Tony and then settled my gaze on his pocket. Silently I walked over to my desk and forcefully snapped my briefcase open. "Were you having a little conversation, my dear?"

"Oh I was just calling Nick's to see if their shipment of artichokes was in." He would not look me in the eye, but was fluttering around the kitchen table straightening silverware.

I looked at him with my most practiced sympathetic look. "Tony, Tony, Tony."

"Wait until you see what you're having tonight."

We silently sat down at the table.

"My dear do I note a little nervousness? Is there something about which you are not being altogether frank? You know that once the covenant of truth is broken, it can never be repaired. How important it is to be straight and true. After all, there are serious consequences to breaking the laws of honesty." Normally I let many peoples' transgressions pass me by with barely a word, but Tony inhabits my terra firma. I had to check my normal legendary tolerance and press the point, for his sake as much as mine. I looked straight into his fleeing eyes and shook my head with solemn and shall we say ominous disappointment.

In his craven agitation he knocked a wine glass over. The sound of shattering glass (I would make sure he reimbursed me for the expense) seemed to trigger futile defiance in his otherwise servile self. "I never go anywhere with you!"

There was a long pause as if it were my fault that he could not accompany me in public. After all it was his own preposterous behavior that made that impossible. Look what happened on Christmas Eve!

Head bowed, hands ineffectually brushing sharp bits

of glass into a pile, I knew he was vanquished when one of those soft hands of his was punctured by a bit of glass; and a red spot, like a tiny spider began spreading its legs across the white table cloth. Fortunately he was carelessly staining his own linen, some frayed family heir loom of his. Like a contrite little boy, he confessed his transgression to me. "That was Sabina on the phone, and she said that we were going to go to her party. I'll buy a new outfit and I'll be very discrete. You'll be proud of me, you'll see."

Placated by the blood draining from his finger, I forgave him, though I never forget transgressions. And yes, my almost bottomless well of compassion was touched by his contrite pliancy. "That should be a lesson to you my boy. Do you not see how confessing the truth makes everything so much more comfortable. Now clean up that mess."

He looked relieved as if a huge weight had been lifted off those shoulders of his. Perhaps I relented too soon, because he immediately stopped his groveling and slipped into an excited, confidential tone. "Do you know Sabina's got a new boyfriend? She met him at that coffee shop, that smoky one I stopped into a while back." Then that annoyingly chatty tone of his dissipated. For an instant, he looked deadly serious. There was one of those strange pauses like time had momentarily fallen and disappeared into a hole. Then he squinted his eyes and once again sank back into his usual foolishness. "She was listening to her friend Bobbie read Sapphic poetry in actual Greek, or was it the Aeneid in Latin? It's been such a long time since I've heard those languages. I think Bobbie wants more than just friendship---poor girl, or boy, whatever she is now."

As if I would want to fill my imagination with the likes of Bobbie Johnson, let alone her Sapphic delights! She is a professor in the Department of Cross Cultural Studies. I didn't even comment on his delusion of knowing Greek and Latin. I detest those new bastard departments: women's Studies, Black Studies, Indian Studies, even Queer studies. What is the world coming to when any ridiculous group of misfits can challenge the sacred canons of western thought? We will slip into the morass of relativism and before we know it, rational law will disintegrate into a Babel of voices in the darkness. With simple dignity I stared tragically at Tony.

As usual he was oblivious to the desperate plight of our civilization. Suddenly once again he was very serious, almost solemn. "I warned her about him. "

I could feel the darkness descend.

Then he was all chatty again. "He's Spanish but his family came from Italy generations ago. Sabina says he's awfully young, but very mature. He has just started opening a whole bunch of coffee shops around the city. He plans to spread his empire across the whole country. And he's going to marry her, Julian, imagine that. Adrian says he's attracted to lesbians, not that Sabina is a lesbian. She told me that she's just bisexual. It must be wonderful to have so many choices. One minute she's going out with Bobbie Johnson and the next, she's marrying an empire builder."

I shook my head sternly. This was all Bobbie's fault. Instead of discretely hiding her deviant sexual proclivities as yours truly does, she goes around talking about matters that best remain unspoken; and when someone like Sabina comes along whose impressionable mind is already addled by mythology; why anything can happen. Perhaps if Bobbie had just remained silent, none of this ensuing story would have happened. Besides she wears plaid, not just any plaid, but ghastly shades of pink and red; a woman of her ungainly stature should avoid being conspicuous.

"Julian, are you listening? It's important that we go.

It may be difficult, but important for both of us." Again he seemed annoyingly serious, almost patronizing. Did I mention that I hate to be patronized?

Like most immature people, if you give Tony an inch, he will take a mile. He was obviously looking for some absolution for his prolonged, calculated betrayal of my trust. Saddened I shook my head. We ate our meal in silence that night. I did not share with him any of my new insights on the amazing transformation of law that occurred between the end of the classical age and the beginning of the medieval. After all there are consequences.

CHAPTER 12

Julian in a white shirt and tie sits haloed by a lamp as he pours over a document in his drab study. The sound of a pan dropping and clanging in the kitchen breaks his concentration. He glances at the clock on the mantel. Its hands are still. He looks toward the kitchen in anger. "Did YOU unplug this?!"

The racket in the kitchen stops. In a casual voice Tony says, "I did what to the June bug? What in the heaven's name are you doing with a June bug this time of year?"

"Christ! What time is it?!"

"About 10:00, I suppose it needs a place for the winter."

Julian stands up, pushing the papers into his briefcase. "Time…you idiot. I asked about the time!"

Tony walks in the dining room, once again with that unearthly serious look on his face. "It's moving faster now. I can feel it."

Exasperated, Julian stares at Tony. "What are you talking about? For once, would you try to make sense?" He stares out the window, exasperated beyond words. Even the window today is opaque with fog.

He snaps his briefcase closed and heads out the door toward campus.

Julian appears like an apparition out of the fog, walking across the campus commons. Dark gray heaps of dirty snow are beginning to melt into messy puddles. Stiffly Julian picks his way along the sidewalk, stiffer than those forlorn new trees that line the commons; spring seemingly still dormant. He doesn't notice the slowly swelling buds.

Sabina and Bobbie appear out of the gloom, walking together, caught in some kind of barely contained argument. Bobbie has a wounded look on her face. Sabina retorts defensively, "I told you that I really wasn't that attracted to you." They almost bump into Julian.

All three stop, disoriented at first.

Sabina more used to chaos, gathers her wits first. "If it isn't the last hope of Western Civilization!"

Julian's look of bewilderment morphs into righteous anger now. "Idiots, idiots, idiots! When will you ever learn?!"

Sabina looks startled by the extent of Julian's anger.

Bobbie protectively steps in front of her. He looks at Julian soulfully. "Life can very heartbreaking."

Julian is again thrown off balance. He stares at Bobbie Incredulously. "Why can't somebody at least try to make sense?"

Sabina chimes in, "Lighten up, this isn't the fall of the Roman Empire." She motions Bobbie to follow her.

Still looking sad, Bobbie follows.

Sabina takes up where she left off. "It's not that I don't like you." She pauses looking directly into Bobbie's eyes. "When I'm with him, I feel magic. I feel like I'm waking up and the world is fantastic. With his love I am the queen of the universe." She suddenly looks away, embarrassed.

Bobbie's eyes redden as she listens to her.

Sabina shakes away her momentary self-consciousness and bristles defiantly. "I want this, I want this so bad. I know he's younger, but I want him. Besides he needs me. He says I am central to his plan."

In the distance Adrian and two frat boys watch. Adrian nods. "Timing is everything."

The two frat boys nod. "We live to serve."

The campus bells toll erratically.

CHAPTER 13

S tore fronts are barely visible through the fog. Street lights flicker on and off and then on again, confused by the murky day. The sluggish whir of cars reverberates through the fog; paired car lights slowly crawl, searching out the road. Inside the dark cars, faces peer through windshields tensely trying to make sense of the day. The sound of tentative footsteps echoes through the fog. Tony appears carrying a large brown paper bag stuffed full. Deep in thought, he stops at a red glowing traffic light. He glances up at it.

He continues to wait there, shifting the bag to his other arm. The whole world seems silent now, frozen. The red light keeps staring unchanged. Tony looks uneasy now.

In the silent distance, strong, steady, purposeful footsteps resound, approaching nearer and nearer. They dominate the whole foggy morning, resounding, approaching. The red light continues to pierce the fog.

In fear and anticipation, Tony turns toward the sound of the footsteps. A large dark form is just barely visible in the distance. It stops. The moment is frozen in complete silence.

Tony whispers into the silence, "I'm not ready yet."

A deep voice whispers, "Soon."

The large form disappears into the fog. Once again the street comes alive with the sound of traffic; car lights continue to search down the street. The traffic light turns green.

CHAPTER 14

I certainly was not looking forward to that mythical jamboree at Sabina's. Not wanting to be overly punitive to Tony, I hardly mentioned to him that this inconvenience was all his fault. After all he was terribly excited. It did the poor dear a wonder of good, though I wish he could have been a little more embarrassed about the trouble that he was causing me. The Saturday evening of the party when he came out of our bedroom all dressed up in a creamy silk shirt with indigo pyramids on it, his hair glowed with a black sheen that would almost look real to an unsophisticated person; his large eyes as shone blue as sapphires, enhanced with just a discrete hint of mascara. I felt proud to have him at my side, or more accurately to have him one step behind.

And of course Sabina had to live on the West Bank. It is a disturbing area caught between the more stately academic halls of the neighboring University of Minnesota and an unfortunate neighborhood of dreary low income high rises. (Why do unfortunates compound their misery by living in such dreary habitats?) Sabina lived in a squalid, old wooden house that should have been torn down for urban renewal, but it suites Sabina, sentimental and wastefully rescued from the past.

In the driveway on that chilly March night I warmed up my BMW with only 40,000 miles on it. As usual Tony lagged behind until I beeped the horn several times. He finally fled the house carrying a large pan covered in aluminum foil. It must be his ubiquitous baklava. I detested the way he covers everything in vast of quantities of aluminum foil. He is absolutely cavalier about his waste of the world's mineral resources; and of course he did not lock the front door of the house. When he finally positioned himself, comfortable and secure with the baklava on his lap I asked, "Now, did you remember to lock the door Tony?" I do not like to accuse people of transgressions, I would much rather ask pointed questions.

He squirmed for a few seconds as if searching for an excuse, and then he appropriately dropped his head in shame and said, "I guess I better go close it." In a last flicker of defiance, he said, "Here, you hold this." There I was holding a sticky pan of baklava on my lap, and my black suite not scheduled to be cleaned for another two months. I hate to take care of other peoples' messes. Perhaps that is the price I pay for being so sweet natured.

As you can imagine I take meticulous care of my car, there I was, thanks to Tony and Sabina, driving my car toward harm's way. As we turned onto the squalid street on which her house precariously perched, I heard the loud tribal voice of some big black woman blaring from an obviously cheap sound system. What served as a primitive melody was bouncing off the walls and out of the window of Sabina's abode...

"R-E-S-P-E-C-T
See how much you mean to me

Sock it to me
Sock it to me."

We stepped in the doorway. The house was filled with people dancing or sharing unfortunate intimacies in dark corners. I could not help it; I gave Tony one last reproachful glance as we descended into the underworld.

Sabina was stationed like a harpy, greeting visitors. She descended upon us. "How wonderful of you to come! Why Tony you look stunning, like a Greek god, and Julian you look your usual grim self. I love that gooey stuff on your pants. Did you and Tony have a quickie before you left home?"

I stared down at my lap, incredulous at the sticky syrup adorning my crotch. I tried to get Tony's attention, to skewer him with a bitter reproach, but he had already put the guilty pan on a table and his body was beginning to tremble and rock with orgiastic bliss..."Sock it to me, Sock it to me." I turned with untarnished dignity to my unruly colleague. She was swathed in some sort of a purple, perhaps vaguely Roman attire. On her head was a tiara. She always overdoes things. "Well my dear I was being gallant to our dear Tony, carrying his gooey Greek offering. This, I pointed to my violated lap, is a badge of courage."

She ignored my riposte. "Hey babe!" She hollered at Tony. "There's someone I want you to meet. Without stopping the rhythmic movements of the pyramids on his shirt, Tony looked up, and smiled such a smile that even I with all my sobriety felt a flutter somewhere in the vicinity of my chest. I felt as if I had never really seen his face before, so vibrant yet so innocent, almost alert; his pouting lower lip no longer protruding beyond his square chin. He did not look afraid. I hate it when he looks afraid; he can be so obsequious.

Now the room that we were in was dismally dark, candles flickering occasionally illuminating writhing bodies. I thought that for a brief second I saw Peder and that wretched Agnes leering at me from the corner like spirits of the dead. I felt myself spinning, loosing precious control as that Black Woman kept wailing. I needed the eternal assurance of light..I needed it. That is when my eyes were drawn to the opening kitchen door, brilliant timeless light streamed through, righting all those slipping, sliding angles of the room. Somehow, I fancied that once again my life had found its clear and steady bearings.

From out of that glorious yellow brilliance appeared a tall, broad shouldered apparition; he seemed to materialize out of the very center of the brightness. For a moment that figure stood in the doorway, beams of light shining from behind and around him like Easter Morning. For some reason I was not troubled that that moment stretched like silly putty, and the music blurred down to deep, wordless, throbbing beats; that glorious figure seemed to mark the center of the world, and I Julian Scribner had found it.

Then it was over; that figure stepped into the more shadowy orgy room; only his eyes held the illumination.

He was dressed in a black leather vest draped over a bare torso, one hair thatched nipple peaked out from a chest that heaved in monumental, heroic breaths. Though I thought that perhaps his attire was rushing spring just a bit, I was taken aback by his pagan splendor. For some strange reason, it hardly registered on me that this was that same collegiate ruffian with whom I had had two previous encounters.

I had never seen Sabina preen before. Even in the undistinguished bloom of her youth, she was after all quite ordinary and downright tomboyish. She actually fluttered as she spoke to him. "Adrian, thank you for joining us; I want to present some people to you." She almost curtsied to him. "This is Julian. He brought Tony who I already told you about."

Adrian nodded at me solemnly as if I had performed some minor but necessary task. I felt those brilliant green eyes of his bore through me and then pass on. I noticed a golden bird dangling from his neck, resting on his naked chest, so much like that silly gift from Tony. I could not remember when I had last seen it…so unusual; my memory has always been such a faithful servant.

Everyone in the room watched him in hushed attendance as he gave Sabina a crisp smile; she must have done her job too. Then Adrian's burning eyes kept moving, seeking something. His gaze reached Tony and stopped. Hadrian stood there motionless as a statue. His fierce eyes seemed to suddenly soften.

Now normally I do not mind if people look at Tony. Though he is a bit worn, he can have a dramatic but fleeting impact, especially in the shadows. Normally under the pressure of lascivious scrutiny Tony glances at me apologetically. Then like a good boy, he retreats to my side. But this time he acted differently. The pyramids on his shirt stopped shaking and without so much as a glance at me, he stood quit transfixed, almost dignified. His eyes shone strangely too; they seemed to catch a golden light. Though they rested on that leather clad and monumental figure, Tony's gaze seemed to stare beyond into some distance that no one else could see. He looked deathly calm perhaps even…sad.

In the previous year of my cozy arrangement with Tony, I had never seen him sad before; petulant, flirtatious, even defiant in small ways, but never sad. Now I saw him looking off towards…through this stranger. Tony's hideously dyed hair, the puffy wrinkles around his eyes, and even that loose flesh under his chin all added to his poignant dignity, dare I say even nobility. His pouting had been replaced by a youthful vulnerability that only sought to understand.

Whatever was happening with Tony, all the rest of us, except Adrian, were on the outside.

Sabina broke the spell. "Adrian, this is Tony." Somehow an introduction seemed unnecessary for those two. A softer beat now filled the room as that black voice started singing,

"Take me to heart

I'll always love you"

The people in the room returned to normal. They huddled together in shadowy groups, listless couples breaking away to cling to each other, dancing slowly. All the while ripples of whispering spread through the room surrounding silent Adrian. No one seemed to notice that I had deigned to make my debut on the party circuit or that It was I who brought this glamorous though slightly faded companion; no one seemed to care that I was there. Even Sabina was too busy staring at Adrian to pay her usual passive aggressive attention to me. I had no one to be oblivious too.

Tony tore his eyes away from Adrian and fled into the kitchen with his gooey pan of baklava, leaving Sabina, myself and this heroic apparition.

Adrian stood as motionless and oblivious as a statue. The brilliance had passed from his eyes. Very humbly Sabina seemed to beg him for a response. "And this is Adrian Ortega." She spoke his name with such pleading veneration. It appeared that she had transferred her devotion from the pot bellied statue on her desk, to this shining male divinity.

Adrian clearly was not my type, much to close to the

earth; besides he had a beard. Unlike my junior colleague, I maintained my composure. I stuck out my hand, not exactly enchanted, but polite. He stood one foot slightly forward. His hands remained at his side. He took a brief glance down at me, nodded imperiously as if I were dismissed, turned to Sabina and simply said, "Splendid." He walked back into the kitchen doorway.

Sabina and I were left there standing alone. The others were busy in the shadows whispering and laughing and caressing each other, but she and I were stranded together somehow bereft. For a moment I was looking from a distance at myself and Sabina…what a pair we looked, myself in a dusty, old, black suite standing straight as a rail and just as severe, and Sabina gaudy and sparkling and for once in her life feeling a bit at a loss. For a moment I felt a hint of something like tenderness for her. "Your friend is certainly impressive, perhaps a bit too hormonal, all that hair you know."

She looked at me for reassurance, like a child lost in a department store looking for help from a stranger. I gave her a little pat on her shoulder and said, "Now where is that Tony? Perhaps he has managed to dump the baklava onto the floor." We both turned toward the kitchen.

As we entered that brilliantly lit kitchen, a confusing sight greeted us. There right next to the dishwasher, Tony was standing absolutely motionless, eyes with that far off look again. Even more bizarre, imperious Adrian was on his knees, pleading some desperate cause. We could see their still profiles as if caught in the marble of some Roman freeze.

I cleared my throat to dispel the preposterous scene. Adrian's body reanimated and without even glancing in my direction the muscles on his barely covered chest began to twitch. He gave Tony one last look and abruptly left the kitchen. Tony's head dropped, but I could see that he was taking rapid, shallow breaths, his face deathly pale. Sabina in a frantic impulse chased after Adrian.

I was just about to tell Tony that this calamity was the direct result of his dishonesty, but then Sabina returned, her tiara tilting dangerously to the left and her face a mask of grief. "He's gone, he's gone; he didn't even tell me where he was going. What did I do wrong?" She stared suspiciously at Tony, her lips tightening. I must say, a bit of an extreme response to Tony's typical foolishness. For the life of me she looked like a jealous empress.

Now I was not sure what was happening, but I knew that we had to maintain decorum at all costs. I took charge, and as if nothing out of the ordinary had occurred, suggested that Tony cut that messy baklava of his, and that Sabina and I begin preparing more hor d'oerves. After all, in case of confusion, revert immediately to the civilized demands of social intercourse.

And sure enough before we knew it, all three of us were very efficiently carrying platters of food out to the throngs as if nothing unusual had happened, and nothing had, you know.

For Sabina's sake I even stayed for the rituals which were only tawdry echoes of the ancient world; thank goodness laws hold their shape better. Though everyone was a buzz with the disappearance of the quest of honor (I do not know why that role had not been assigned to me, after all what is one rather inarticulate mesomorph compared to yours truly), I as usual maintained my quiet dignity. The world of fools is stirred with drama; the course of my life runs in harmonious order.

As we left that fiasco that I had valiantly attempted to keep in order, I noticed how that particular color of blue suited Tony, not that I actually told him so, after all there are bounds to my generosity. I did remind him though about the bonds of faithfulness. After all one can never be reminded of those restrictions too often. "Faithfulness, Tony, scrupulous faithfulness is essential if a person wants to continue in my company."

Tony nodded at me obliviously; he was back to his usual self. "What a fun party, Julian. Those people you work with are wonderful, all so interested in all those long ago stories. I really didn't get much of a chance to talk with Sabina. I loved her outfit. She was so busy she hardly had time to talk with me."

"Your baklava was better than usual my dear."

"I'm sorry about your suite."

"You were quite fetching tonight, if I must say so myself."

"Does that mean you'll take me along again sometime?"

"Perhaps, but not for a while. I will have to send this suite to the cleaner ahead of schedule."

All things right in my world, I drove us home down Franklin Ave.

CHAPTER 15

The same evening...Adrian, still dressed in Roman attire as he had been at the party, stands silently in the doorway of the fraternity house living room, listening. One of the young men sprawled out in a beaten up, overstuffed chair holds a beer. "I just don't get. " He stares directly at Adrian.

The other young men except for the speaker notice Adrian.

The young man continues speaking loudly and sarcastically. "What's the deal getting together with that old bag. She's not even hot. He doesn't even like her...what's this shit about marrying her?"

The other young men glance at Adrian uneasily.

The young man suddenly notices Adrian in the doorway.

Adrian locks his gaze on the young man. Time is at a standstill.

Adrian turns away; the young man shifts uneasily in his chair and nervously takes a swig of beer.

The other men in the room turn towards him now staring with cold hostility.

Fear and guilt and anger filter through the young man's

face. He shoots a frightened hostile look at everyone in the room. "I didn't mean it. You go ahead and do what you want. See if I care."

Adrian turns to the young man briefly , a slight smile on his lips. "That's not enough."

"I mean, I didn't mean to say anything. It's fine by me." He is visibly shaking.

Adrian looks at the others. "It's fine by him. It's fine by him." He starts laughing brutally.

All the watchers start laughing as if on signal.

The young man stands IP and starts backing away from the circle, leaving his beer can behind. "I'll do whatever you want. It was just a lousy opinion….I'm sorry man, I'm sorry."

Subtly the group is closing in on the young man as he moves away.

Adrian looks at his cohorts smiling. "He says he has an opinion." The whole group breaks out in vicious laughter.

The young man flees the room in panic, knocking over a chair.

Adrian, totally calm, motions to one of the laughing men. "I don't want to see his face again."

One of the young men mutters menacingly, ""That asshole just doesn't get it. He needs someone to teach him a lesson."

The whole group suddenly becomes quiet, eyes focused on Adrian.

Order complete, Adrian moves on. "I have something to do tonight."

A couple of the guys chime in. "Can we help you boss."

"Who did I give Julian's address to?"

A young man nods and says, "Now there's a real asshole."

Adrian sticks his hand out to no one in particular. A

young man scrambles around in his pocket and pulls out a wad of paper. Adrian nods imperceptibly. With desperate gratitude on his face the young man puts it in Adrian's hand.

CHAPTER 16

A cold night, a lone car, windows an opaque black, slowly drives down Franklin Ave., lights shining on the desolate road…Julian's car.

A drunk couple stagger out of one of the bars. One of them collapses on the cold sidewalk. The other groggily stares at his fallen comrade. Finally he bends over and tries to pull his companion up. They both fall back to the sidewalk and simply lie there.

The car moves on up the street.

Three blocks up a young girl with no jacket on runs down the street frantically, silently.

She pauses just long enough to look back, then keeps running.

Julian's car pauses for a moment and then drives on into the night.

CHAPTER 17

As I drove up Franklin Ave after the party, Tony was quiet. Now normally I love quiet; quietness is so steady, controlled; but that night, I don't know, that night I felt an emptiness in my stomach. As I looked out on the street, there was a lone frightened girl running, just running. Someone had obliviously forgotten to tell her to dress warmly. I wish the people who lived down here were more careful. I almost stopped to find out what was wrong, but I decided it was none of business.

I realized that I did not want to talk about that party, but simply to slip back into the routine that I had so carefully established with Tony. I never realized how comfortable it was, even that stale breath of his in the morning. He really should brush his teeth more often, after all when one gets to be his age, one just ought to.

When we got out of the car, he smiled at me, embarrassed, as if he were reading my thoughts. Our feet crunched on the last of the winter snow. The sounds echoed out into the clear cold dark; stars crinkled back.

We stepped onto the enclosed porch filled with piles of old newspapers. I unlocked the heavy wooden door into the safety of my abode. Tony followed in tow with a strange almost dazed shuffle. Now normally I am in bed by 9PM ; I hate it when my routine is disturbed. Immediately proceeding up the stairs I hung up my suite and turned off the light. Instead of facing the restful dark of night, the room was filled with the glow of the newly risen moon. Normally I face sleep with a deep sense of satisfaction...all is right with me world; all is as it should be. But that night I crawled into bed with my underwear on and closed the covers over me like a shadowy cocoon, as if I were looking for safety, or even worse as if something were about to change.

Tony followed me into the bedroom, his steps padding in. I felt him sit on the edge of the bed. I peered through a crack in the covers and watched him pull off his shoes and socks. After setting those more prosaic accouterments on the floor, he sat stone still there on the edge of the bed. Usually my Tony is a creature of drama, continually casting glances at his audience, but tonight he seemed oddly composed. He quietly stood up and as if drawn by the moonlight; he walked toward the window. A huge swollen moon was rising and casting its livid light through the window and onto Tony. Now, I am not a person of whimsy let alone compulsion, but I felt this odd urge to call him back from the window as if some danger awaited him. Yet I felt so powerless underneath all those protective covers. All I could do was watch his strange moonlit dance. Yes, if it was a dance, a dirge, his gestures graceful and yet somehow sad. Delicately he unbuttoned that silk shirt of his with the blue pyramids. How clear I could see those pyramids in the moonlight. His shirt hung loose and shimmering. Then in what seemed like a sensuous reflex, his body arched up and into a backwards curve. The glow of the moon found his white chest exposed as his shirt shimmered off his shoulders and onto the floor behind him in a soft whisper of pleasure.

Now he stood in alabaster profile against the night. Brushing his chest to a fine sheen, the cold fingers of the moon lingered lovingly on his nipples until they stuck straight out like two little nubs.

For a moment the dreamy mood was dispelled as he nervously glanced out the window. I felt somehow reassured by his more familiar melodrama. For a moment I wondered who was out there, but then restrained my curiosity. Why spoil this delightful little performance surely meant for my eyes alone. His chest rose with a deep breath. He stood there in frozen suspense, and just when I began becoming alarmed at his stillness, he released a sigh, a long drawn out note both sweet and sad. With the slightest push of his right hand, his pants and underwear dropped to the ground. His keys jangled like a temple bell. How well my Tony looked in the moon light.

Then he turned moving toward me; his shadowy form so quiet. I was still peering secretly from between the covers. I know that this is an undignified thing for some one like me to be doing, but the moonlight seemed to be having a strange affect on me. He walked over to the bed and lifted the covers to reveal me, wide eyed and watching. Then he crouched down and gave me a little kiss, as if I were some dear but obtuse child. Oddly, despite being treated in such a misguided and patronizing way, I felt a strange excitement. Now as everyone surely knows, I am a tender and generous man, to a fault even, but to respond to him with such fervor…I do not know what happened. My heart it almost ached, and my under wear bottoms were tented with excitement. The pressure was uncomfortable. Gently as if he could read my thoughts, he slipped the offending garment down my legs and off my feet leaving my penis hard and throbbing in the eerie moonlight.

Now, normally love making for Tony is very serious occupation indeed, transforming submission into a fine art. At first with a funny little smile on his face, he would tease me with little kisses on my face, neck, and on my hairless but well defined chest (those calisthenics have done wonders). His lips then would begin working their irrevocable journey down across that stomach of mine which I have taken such pains to keep firm. Then his flicking tongue would continue traveling lower still until he would nestle his face into my groin. Finally with consummate skill he would nibble around the cap of my pencil hard penis (I have often mentioned to Tony how smaller cocks get harder and have more staying power). With a little slurp of a sucking sound, my penis already hard (it knows what is coming next, or perhaps it know it is coming next) would propel itself into his soft moist, hopefully yearning mouth. When I would be ready and he had completed his artful activity, Tony would suddenly stop and lie flat on his back, spreading his legs beckoning me with an exaggerated look of need. I would gallop like a horse to the trough. While his eyes were wide open I would enter him with a little shove. He would wince and then smile. At this point he would start talking about the price of olive oil or some new face cream. At first it bothered me, his coy dispassion, but soon I grew to enjoy being the object of his occupation.

But that strange moonlit night, he lay there on the bed beside me, propped up on one elbow, watching me silently. Our breathing seemed to steady and come together into a single rhythm. For the life of me, there was something wise and almost ageless about the way he looked. Then he slipped his hand under my head. I felt cradled there. He rested his head back on the pillow and with gentle but clear pressure he pulled me onto him. His eyes were closed; his lips moist and slightly parted. I watched him for a moment in the glow of that night, quick silver running through me.

I slipped on top of him and kissed his warm, open mouth. I don't know what got into me. Generally in the past, I eschewed kisses, particularly the sloppy wet kind.

Then pressing my lips to his left tit, I suckled…what a strange sensation. Slowly reaching down to grab his buttocks, his body tensed and then shivered into a relaxed receptivity that I had never experienced from him before. I pushed my head and shoulders up to make sure that this was my artful Tony. Sure enough the face was familiar but his closed eyelids flickered in some uncalculating, blind passion. If I must say so myself I was really out doing myself that night raising Tony to unheralded heights. Finally I pushed myself between his legs. They rose up almost by themselves, presenting me with the luscious target of my pleasure. I played with the lip of his anus with my excited but unusually patient cock. Ever so slowly like tide rising, did I feel drawn in; I was tenderly swallowed inch by inch until we seemed like one ocean. He was moaning now in a kind of a rhythmic unintelligible chant, eyes still sealed shut, his body underneath me churning. His hips kept thrusting up hungry for more.

Now normally I am very cautious with my orgasms. I like to feel the pleasure and hold on to it. I can punch that trusty penis of mine in and out for hours, slowly letting the semen drip out with no messy explosion. That way I prolong the pleasure and at the same time maintain control. But as Tony's body pulled me in, those long moans fueling my excitement, something in my very gut seemed to swell up and finally burst, rushing through my whole body. Suddenly before I had time to clench, I had emptied out into Tony, my love.

As I exploded so did he. His lips let out a long forlorn and desperate cry, and whispered something that I could not understand. He opened his eyes and for a moment looked startled to see that it was I, Julian Scribner, leaning over him. He studied my features with a mysterious tenderness, certainly in a way that no one had ever looked at me before, and then gently rose from the bed and walked into the bathroom.

My whole self spent, I sank into the bed and immediately into a well deserved sleep. After a few minutes or a few hours, I do not know which since the clock in the bedroom had once again stopped, I woke up with a start as if something had nudged me. What was it that Tony whispered in his ecstasy? I turned toward his still form, but decided not to wake him. Maybe it was just my aching full bladder, I got out of bed and stood up; for some curious reason I glanced out of the window. The moon was higher in the sky, smaller, a bleak and icy marble, and there standing in the street was Adrian. His breath puffing steam, his burly arms stretched out motionless toward the house. In the cold darkness, his bare chest underneath his vest glowed. He did not move. Except for the steam around his head I would have thought it was a statue, some heroic personification of yearning or perhaps despair. I walked into the bathroom, turned on the light, and pissed the mystery away; I flushed it all down. When I walked back into the bedroom Tony was asleep on his accustomed spot, and the street was clear.

What an extraordinary dream! I crawled into bed and kissed him on his closed eyes and fell asleep again. In the morning I hardly remembered my fantasy; after all dreams can make fools of anyone, perhaps even me.

CHAPTER 18

E arly spring morning, a robin calls. The skies burst into songs of yearning and warning. Even students become animated, and hope rises like the sap in those meager trees that line the sidewalk around the campus mall..

Bobbie was stands in Julian and Sabina's empty office, lost in thought as he gazes at the bust of Hadrian the Magnificent. His sorrow is conspicuous on this glorious morning. Shyly he touches the figure with a finger of his right hand. He winces and quickly pulls his finger back.

Julian marches in. He looks ever so slightly distracted, his mask of composure ever so slightly frayed. Unpacking his briefcase, he notices Bobbie standing next to the bust. Julian looks startled, by the invasion. He glances at Bobbie with barely contained hostility. "To what do I owe this pleasure? You may go merrily bumping into to things outside this office, but watch your step here, particularly around that statue." His fixes his eyes on Bobbie, "Really!"

Bobbie looks down timidly. "No…well yes…I came to see her…I mean Sabina…then I just found myself looking at the statue."

Julian bristles. "Have you ever heard of syntax? Words

actually do go together in sentences, at least in this department. Beside, I would like you to know that, that statue is not just any statue. It's the bust of Hadrian the Magnificent. He was a true marvel, an architect, administrator, poet, philosopher, law giver..." Julian is getting carried away.

There is an edge of anger in Bobbie's voice; he interrupts, his voice going to lower register. "He was still human just like the rest of us, making mistakes, suffering, shitting and dying." He glances with contempt at the statue. "That's just stone, cold stone, and even that will crumble some day."

Julian is shaken, at a loss for words.

Bobbie watches, his face softening. "I was out of line. I have no right to come in here and insult this thing...just because..." Her eyes begin reddening, her big innocent face starts to twitch. Once again the campus bells sound. "I wish someone would fix the clocks around her." She turns away.

Julian perked up. "You notice it too?"

Bobbie nods. "It's like time is getting mixed up."

"Some of Julian's anger dissipates. "I thought I was the only one."

"She doesn't want to talk with me...not even see me anymore." Her face starts scrounging up.

A momentary glimmer of softness passes across Julian's face. "I just don't know what got into her. You know how young or not so young lovers are." Julian stops unsure of what to say.

Bobbie glances at Julian. "I'm just not...you know, the hero type. I'm a bit player." She stares earnestly at Julian now. "You know what I mean."

All softness disappears from Julian's face. 'Surely you don't think that about me? I am an important person around here."

Bobbie shakes his head sadly, "Important?"

Julian looks bewildered.

Sabina pushes into the room. She ignores Bobbie and shoots an angry imperious glance at Julian. "What did you do to him, you and that bitch boy of yours?"

The three are a frozen tableau until Peder stuck his head in the doorway. "Boys will be boys." He laughs maliciously, knowingly.

Sabina looks shocked and then shutters; her imperious airs evaporate, leaving a lonely frightened girl.

Bobbie watches.

Late afternoon, dark clouds are shouldering out spring, leaving the air blustery and cold. Bobbie steps out onto the Commons glancing around uneasily. She puts her collar up and heads off in the direction of the library building.

She sits at a computer; students mill around her at other computers in the library. Bobbie doesn't notice. She starts, punching keys, looking up random words…"Hadrian," "Rome," "reincarnation," "Mythology." She keeps going deeper and deeper, curious, baffled, frustrated. Then she starts wondering around the stacks of old books.

She hears soft humming from somewhere in the stacks.

An old woman, looking very much like the bag lady and the old slave woman, is dusting the books…yes she is the one humming.

At first Bobbie avoids her and moves to another part of the stacks, but wherever she went that strange humming sound follows.

The old woman finally approaches him. "You're here late, is there something that I can help you with?"

Bobbie startles in confusion. "Nothing…nothing."

She looks at him directly. "Are you sure?"

Bobbie turns away, embarrassed but finally curiosity

prevails. "What's that tune you are humming? It sounds so familiar."

"Oh that. Its a child's lullaby. It goes like this. Row, row, row you're boat gently down the stream, merrily merrily, merrily, merrily, life is but a dream." She pauses as if looking for some familiar response.

Bobbie backs away slightly. "A lot of good that'll due me."

The old woman smiles tenderly at her. "You never know."

Bobbie cocks her head and continues to stand there for the longest time.

When she finally steps out of the library, it is now dark and wintry. The cutting wind rips at her clothes. There is an unusual sense of purpose to her steps as she disappears into the night.

CHAPTER 19

Perhaps Tony and that foolish family of his have some genetic flaw. Somehow a gene responsible for logical thought has been replaced by some mutant gene that can only produce preposterous fancy. How grateful I am that science is finally recognizing that thoughts and feelings are simply the fuzzy reflection of very orderly and logical chemical reactions that we have the opportunity, or rather the obligation to control. The stage is set for someone with the brilliance of Hadrian to create an orderly system based on chemical reactions that will encompass all human experience and behavior. Did I mention (excuse me for the possible repetition; though I'll only admit this to you, of late I have begun forgetting things) Tony has a family. Some months after I found Tony living with me, on Sunday morning, and in fact every Sunday morning thereafter, those strange people flock to my doorway. That first Sunday morning I was busy exploring Vatican encyclicals of the 18th century for traces of the Edict Perpetuam. I do admire popes; how wise it is of them to be oblivious to current cultural fads and assert unquestioningly the divine authority embodied in themselves. I am very concerned about peoples' disregard for the sacredness of authority. There is an infallibility of order that only refined and clear thinking people can recognize. It is our duty to impose that order on the muddle headed masses. Though I have some concerns about the religious context of papal infallibility, I think order must be maintained at all costs.

I heard pounding at the door. The fact that my doorbell has not worked for 15 years is not an inconvenience; it keeps the riffraff away. Imagine if I were to be disturbed by every salesman, Jehovah Witness, or child selling overpriced candy bars for his school football team; but the knocking continued in annoying determination.

Since Tony's wisdom is always in doubt, I did not ask him earlier that morning why he was frantically skittering around in the kitchen making huge quantities of some sort of egg dish with much too much garlic. Was this some sort of contest to see how many dozens of eggs he could waste? Or was he cooking for a whole ravenous army...the ways of Tony are indeed mysterious. In this case though, I underestimated his absurdity. As usual, I was too generous.

The knocking was climaxing to a banging crescendo. I deigned to look up and to my surprise I saw a Lilliputian male pounding at my door with feverish delight. Normally I would have ignored the commotion or called the police, but Tony ran to the door with the embracing arms of welcome. He frantically threw the door wide open as if he could not see that person soon enough; a gust of wind blew some of my piled manuscripts across the floor. Rightly I decided to ignore the intrusion, although Tony and I would discuss this later.

That very small man stood at the opened door. Tony was bubbling over in excitement, "Jerome! It's wonderful to see you! And you're looking so..."

Tony paused for a moment as if he were at a loss to

describe how this apparition looked. "You're looking so fabulous, absolutely fabulous!"

Even from my vantage point, camouflaged behind my desk, I could see that Tony's use of this descriptor was unfortunate. I would have used a decidedly less complementary word...*strange*, *bizarre*, or perhaps *lunatic*. But after all, I see things so much clearer than Tony. The little man barely acknowledged Tony's overly effusive greeting and simply charged into my house. He may have given Tony a passing wink; I could not tell because I really was not supposed to be looking.

Even at 9 AM, it was still a cool morning, but I could feel the blistering heat radiated by this little dynamo. I deigned to look up. His cheeks were flushed with some internal furnace that had already singed any suggestion of hair from his head. His eyes were like little glowing coals ready to burst into flame right in front of me. I was concerned about my valuable papers. His face was like a skull, much too large for his tiny frame. Any soft flesh had been burned off to maintain the furnace of his unearthly intensity.

He noticed me and shot sparks in my direction. Focusing the entire energy of those glowing eyes on me, he grinned. Dry thin lips stretching in a ghoulish approximation of a smile, revealed a whole set of very white sharp teeth. He had found his target and shot right to my desk, urgently slamming down a cheap plastic briefcase on my precious research. Unsuccessfully attempting to undue the latch (When will people learn that you always get what you pay for?), he finally, igniting with impatience, viciously punching the belly of the case. It sprung open spewing its entire lurid contents onto my orderly desk.

"Now Julian, may I call you Julian?"

He did not pause to let me say "no."

"What you see before you are important test results. The National Office of Nutritional Efficacy, a not for profit organization of which I had no small part in founding, has proven BEYOND all possible shadow of doubt that wheat grass grown in the magnificent Orono valley in upstate Maine has properties particular and efficacious that the whole world needs now. Did you hear me, NOW!"

I am known for my bravery and resourcefulness under fire, but he was holding the entire invaluable contents of my desk hostage with his incendiary remarks. Wisely I nodded.

"There are minerals up there that are no where else in the world, trace minerals that we don't even have names for, but by god we need them. YOU need them. We all need them." His wiry, little body convulsed with a burst of energy that was supposed to be a laugh.

I reached to pull my valuable manuscripts away from danger, but before I could even touch my threatened papers, he plunged into his back pocket and pulled out a smashed mass of something that was wrapped in metallic green paper.

Julian, you MUST try this right now. I promise you it will change your life!" He shoved that hot metallic mass into my hand.

I looked at it in disbelief, and began for the sake of my threatened papers and their importance to posterity to open that revolting packet. After all I smelled fire and brimstone on his breath.

Evidently my progress in disinterring whatever was inside was too slow for the frenzied Jerome. He erupted like a miniature volcano. "Julian DON'T fiddle with that wrapper. Your life is at stake: eat it right NOW!" Just then my desperate fingers managed to tear through an end of the wrapper. I felt both relief and horror, after all, now I who had been so careful about the purity of my diet would have to eat the gooey greenish brown thing that emerged. Alas, what I do for the sake of posterity. Any false move on my part and my research would go up in smoke. What a tragedy for the human race!

The contents of the wrapper were as warm as the droppings of a canine, not that I had ever really touched that filth. As you can see my carefully bridled imagination was being stoked by the threatening frenzy of this intruder... and this was happening in my house, my refuge! Just then I was able to slip the most precious of my papers out from under that briefcase. As the goo was beginning to melt in my hand, I decided that I was finally ready to give Jerome a piece of my mind and if necessary use my well trained muscles to show him who was really the boss here.

Just then I heard a kind of slow slapping at the door. Tony ran to the door gasping, "It must be Cleo."

On my front steps stood a bizarre looking gypsy of a woman, covered in bangles and veils. She had a gauzy crimson blouse on with what looked like the design of a snake curling around one of her overblown bosoms. Tony opened the door and then knelt as this personage stood like a reigning queen in the doorway. "You can stand up now darling Tony."

Why is it that everyone in that family always seems to be caught in mid act? Every entrance was the continuation of an already progressing scene. The sound of tinkling jewelry and the heavy smell of musk permeated the room as she stepped in sniffing and smiling lasciviously. "Hormones, male hormones, I smell them, how delightful." Her nose seemed to lead her wafting body in a gentle curve to the site of my heroic last stand. Looking back and forth from Jerome and to yours truly, her eyes narrowed, and her nostrils flared; she began breathing heavily. With sudden and surprising power she grabbed diminutive Jerome by his ears lifting him off the ground. "So you're up to your own tricks you dogmatic pig. I love it!"

Jerome wiggled in either delight or rage, with that death's head face of his I could never tell.

Dropping him, she left him to scurry into the corner. She backed towards my desk, and before I had time to take protective measures, she settled her voluptuous bottom on that otherwise sober site of so many of my important intellectual ventures. One buttock rested on Jerome's important test results, the other buttock, alas, settled on those manuscripts that I had just salvaged. Once again I was caught in an uninvited quandary; after all her body was damp and saturated with oily scent.

"Jerome, you mustn't scare our new in-law away." She settled herself a little more comfortably on my papers and turned towards me licking her lips. "My, Julian you look absolutely compelling, all sweaty and desperate, ready to have one of your little macho tiffs."

For a moment I was outraged that she could characterize the courageous protection of my manuscripts, indeed my valorous protection of all western thought, as a little macho tiff. Though her obvious attraction to me certainly was an indication of good taste, she too, like the rest of the family was still prone to poor judgment. Besides, I could almost feel that musky film of perfume that covered her body soaking into my research.

While smiling gallantly at her, I attempted to casually slip my papers out from underneath her with my left hand. She appeared to have felt that papery friction on her oily bottom, and began caressing my hand. "Aren't you the eager one? Lucky Tony."

Why, I was aghast that this obvious harlot would think

that someone of my fine cultivation would be interested in her tawdry charms. I continued to smile; after all I had my papers to guard. She must have mistaken my hostage smile for an invitation and began tracing little seductive circles on my sweaty palm. Grabbing one of my fingers she pulled it with a repetitious throbbing motion, all the while smiling at Tony who (that traitor) seemed absolutely oblivious to the outrages being perpetrated on my personage and possessions. Only later would I understand that the benighted treatment that I suffered was a matter of course for that most foolish of families. How vulgar! They are like so much of humanity. All I have to do is look at that family to understand what the world would be like without we few lonely beacons of righteousness like yours truly.

Now I felt the fingers of her oily hand gradually crawling up my arm towards my more tender flesh. "You'll have to excuse Jerome. These Fathers of the Church, they're so single minded you know, always trying to press their point. I know that you, Julian, are more interested in pressing more pleasurable points. Don't you think so Tony?"

This time she did not wait for an answer. Totally engrossed in playing with the soft tissue on the underside of my upper arm, she did not bother to look up. Even with a body as finely toned as mine, there are still hidden areas of soft almost flabby flesh.

I was caught in a conundrum. In fact I did not know why or how any of this was happening. By some clever feat of dexterity her entire hand had now worked itself up my sleeve (If only I had not given in to the vagaries of the weather and worn a short sleeved shirt that morning). Her fingers now were curling in the sparse hair of my under arms. My face under unbelievable duress must have betrayed some consternation.

She gave that hair a little tug to get my attention. "Why, Julian you don't have a clue do you? Even though you think you're so brilliant, you don't understand a thing yet do you? Poor dear! I suppose Tony has been too busy getting his bum basted to explain anything yet. You certainly have a tight little body for an old man." She retrieved her hand from my arm pit and was pinching my biceps while making little moaning sounds.

If I do say so myself my biceps are rather impressive... from all my push ups. I ignored her foolish comment about age. As usual, just when that poor girl began expressing her appreciation for the finer things of life, she again demonstrated her ignorance.

Very intimately she began whispering in my ear. "This is the age of recycling. You of all people should know about recycling. Recycle your cans, your plastic, your glass, your newspapers. By the way, what ARE you doing with all those newspapers piled around the porch?" She did not wait for an answer. "Why, I don't want to be too obvious my dear and insult your intelligence about which I have heard so much; let me just say that..." She paused and smiled knowingly.

It was becoming clear to me that I was in a room filled with madmen, or to be politically correct, mad persons (although I know that all this focus on being politically correct is just a hidden ploy to indulge in chaos). Even my normally docile Tony was a player in this bedlam; he kept putting his finger to his mouth making shushing sounds at Cleo. Then he would burst into laughter.

Despite Tony's ridiculous attempt to quiet her, Cleo literally pressed on; her hand pushing into my chest. "Why Jerome over there, is THE Jerome, saint and father of the Catholic Church. He did his best to stomp out any of those nasty old pagans. He also had quite an appetite for heretics.

Very persuasive man he was, although a little dangerous, if you catch my drift. Poor boy, lately, no one feels strong enough about Christianity to actually burn people at the stake, so he's become a multilevel marketer of nutritional supplements. It is a bit of a let down."

For a moment I was actually seduced into feeling sympathy for that pip squeak.

"And I, I am Cleopatra, the queen."

She must have taken my heavy breathing for some sort of invitation to continue.

"Not that I moved immediately from THAT Cleopatra, to this recycled Cleopatra. I was a rather randy abbot in the 9th century, and then I was a Arab girl who died at the age of fourteen in the fall of Antioch in the 12th century…I was raped and gutted by a crusader. In the 19th Century I tried a new gig. I was Marie Curie…all that radium did me in. So, I decided to come back in a body closer to the prototype. I do look marvelous don't I?"

I nodded as the pressure of my pencil penis pushed uncomfortable against my zippered pants.

Her tongue flicked out like an adder into my ear. "Now Tony here is the male beauty of the family, a real ephebe. He's got a delicious history. He was the beautiful…"

Suddenly her face and those of her two brothers turned with sudden awe to the portal of the front door. There was no knocking this time. The door swung open it seemed by itself, revealing the most disturbing looking figure of them all. She had a blue veil on with a diadem of sparkling stars. In both hands she held plastic snakes. Her body was clothed in gauzy fabric revealing a very rotund and large breasted figure very much like Sabina's pot bellied goddess. As a finishing touch, she had a rosary strung around her waist. She stepped through the door, lifted the snakes so that her arms were raised like a Cretan goddess. In unison all three siblings said, "MOTHER" and dropped to their knees... shear bedlam. In that moment of relative calm I realized that this was that insane bag lady I had seen on the streets what seemed so long ago. At least I think so…my brain, my brain…I'm not as clear headed any more.

She smiled a soft, sad smile and waved her arms over not only them, but also myself (as if I bore some similarity to those other lunatics) and said, "My children." Then she simply stood there motionless. I experienced one of those annoying little wrinkles of time, silence stretching out. It could have lasted a second or a lifetime; finally I was ushered back into my usual and thankfully more sane reality by the sound of a truck shifting gears on the street outside.

Tony then took charge. "Time for breakfast! I've made this wonderful omelet with goat cheese and garlic. You know how they make it in Corinth."

Jerome seemed to have forgotten about his test results; Cleopatra pulled her hand off my chest; and Mother dropped her snakes. They all rushed to the kitchen, chattering.

I stayed stationed at my desk to let the excitement in my loins subside. I had not had this problem since grade school. Tony stuck his head around the corner and with the most heart rending pout on his lips that I had yet to witness, he whispered. "Julian, hurry up, c'mon it's not so bad, breakfast will get cold." Then he winked at me and said, "My family likes you. Cleo thinks you're delicious, but you know how she is about Romans."

I knew Tony was a lost cause; I did not correct him about my parentage. The Scribners are a fine English family with a legal bent who came over on the Mayflower. Tony is so suggestible. We would talk about this later, we certainly would. Although I must admit for the briefest of moments standing in the dim hallway to the kitchen he looked nubile and almost adolescent. I got up and followed him, noticing a fetching sway to his hips, nothing too blatant like his sister, but simply willowy. Then he walked me over to the empty seat between Cleo and Jerome. So great is my tolerance for human frailty that I treated my guests with hospitality. They seemed so pleased that I was among them, as if they knew me.

The conversation at that table skidded crazily over the centuries. I learned the latest gossip from Athens, Constantinople, Baghdad, and Troy. In order to anchor that conversation to sanity, I began explaining the significance of Roman law to the Magna Carta, they all listened enthralled as if it were some breaking news.

Jerome nodded his head toward me and said, "After all where would the Church be without Roman hierarchy and order. Those Romans, so good at punishment; they made it into a science. Although the Church did them one better; it made punishment eternal…how terrible, how wonderful!"

Cleo winked at Tony, "Don't you wish your pal Hadrian had stuck to turning boys into gods instead of making all those dusty laws. By the way, have you started taking swimming lessons yet?"

Jerome's death heads face leered at Tony. Or was he simply smiling? "Getting ready for your big splash. Eh Tony?"

Tony's head almost dropped into his fragrant Greek omelet.

The chatter at the table stopped; Tony seemed strangely disturbed. Under the table Cleo brushed my inner thigh with her fingers. Jerome leaned over towards me; I could feel his fiery breath on my ear. "Depraved sodomites always get their due."

Mother looked around the table, at all of us as if we were

quarreling siblings. "Now children, I don't want any of this teasing. Why Tony here was the last of his kind."

This seemed to be some sort of signal; simultaneously all three uninvited guests wiped their mouths, stood up, and proceeded out the door. They did not even say goodbye to each other. Despite their lunacy, there was something oddly predictable about their behavior that perhaps made hello's and goodbye's extraneous. As I was considering whether I was giving the family undue credit for logic, Tony kept jangling around the kitchen, humming some melody in a minor key as if nothing unusual had happened. I thought if I kept grimly sitting at the table he would say something... some kind of explanation or apology.

When he pulled my half eaten and now cold omelet from under my nose, he said, "Goat cheese a little strong for you? I know that Roman stomachs are notorious delicate, no sense of daring."

What could I do? Whatever I would say would give credence to this preposterous morning. I too would become a player in the absurdity. I finally settled for silence. Tony and I never talked about it, except that every Sunday morning thereafter they would all appear, eat, and then be gone.

CHAPTER 20

Dark, except for the faint yellow sickly glow of a street light outside…an unintelligible voice, a youthful voice calls out in a strange mishmash of languages. A tone of desperate pleading sadness rings through the layers of language and into the night.

Slowly the moon starts edging across the window. Lying on his back, Julian's eyes spring open. His startled eyes reflect a glimmer of the moonlight as he lies there motionless, like a frightened child at night.

The words, those pleading words keep poring out into the darkness.

The moon now is in the window watching.

Julian with great effort breaks the spell and grimaces. He jerks his head up and then cautiously looks over at Tony as he lies naked on his back, pleading to the moon.

Julian rises on his elbow listening, trying to sort out meaning. He catches bits of Latin and Greek, but even those fragments are intermixed with sounds and words that he can not decipher. He listens…

As the moon edges out of view, Tony's pleading voice stops abruptly. He looks abandoned and hopeless. Suddenly his body trembles as he takes a big gasp of air. His eyes are frozen open now as his chest stops moving. After a convulsive shutter he appears lifeless, floating in the darkness.

Julian watches in paralyzed horror. A lone dog howls in the distance.

Time empties out.

Suddenly Tony grimaces in pain and takes a sharp ragged breath, he open his eyes staring out blankly into the distance. Then he closes his eyes and once again begins taking the measured breaths of sleep.

Julian watches. Then his eyes close and he too sleeps.

Like naked babies Julian and Adrian lie next to each other in the darkness.

Julian wakes up the next morning strangely tired, his face worn with anxiety and regret. As Tony lies in bed sleeping, Julian drags himself through his morning routines. The world outside his window is a blank opaque gray as if the usual world had disappeared leaving only confusion.

His usual day…shadowy car after shadowy car crawl through the beating rain, there lights straining to make sense of the deluge. Julian, a mere shadow sits in his car watching the windshield wipers hopelessly trying to clear the windshield. As rain continues to beat against the car he desperately clutches the steering wheel.

The electric clock flashes numbers, changing by the second, as if yesterday, today and tomorrow were foolish delusions. He urgently stares into the rear view mirror whispering, "Every day in every way, I am becoming better and better." His wild eyes strain to look out,

His headlights shine on the back of a car directly in front of him. On the bumper is written, "IT IS LATER THAN YOU THINK!"

CHAPTER 21

I never talked about those breakfasts with anyone. What would I say?...that Cleopatra, St. Jerome, and some demented earth goddess pay a visit ever Sunday and seem to think that Tony and I have some part in their madness? Besides they kept changing names. Lately Tony was calling Mother, Sophie. I suppose I could have exiled Tony and his family from my life, but I had come to enjoy Greek cooking and needed my boy-man, Tony. The lunacy must have been contagious because there were times after those breakfasts, so saturated by their foolishness was I, that I felt that I too had some kind of part to play in the proceedings, something that I needed to do...as if I had left something undone. I needed to remind myself that I never leave anything unfinished.

In fact over the ensuing months even the most bizarre behavior perpetrated by students or freeway drivers by comparison to that unholy family's mad cap seemed insignificant if not normal. I began tolerating absurdity in my life. I never thought I would use that word to describe anything in which I was involved. I think toleration of absurdity began at that first meeting with Tony and was one of the reasons I actually went to that fateful spring fete at Sabina's. Even when Sabina was overwhelmed by the mystery of Adrian's sudden disappearance, I was to say the least, not troubled. Was I loosing my edge?

Besides Adrian's disappearance seemed far less mysterious than his determination to wed my unglamorous junior colleague. As for Sabina, her behavior was strictly déclassé. Why did not she follow the example of yours truly and be discrete about her relationship. Fortunately I'm not the one who has to sleep with that brute.

I tried to contain my life in its careful rhythms; of course there was that little problem with the dimension of time. I had already become used to clocks stopping and moments stretching, but then I began having trouble with my depth perception. It is not simply that my parallel parking was no longer as precise as it used to be, but I found myself bumping into people or even worse into walls. Though I hate to dissemble, I was forced to explain to the witnesses of my misadventures that I needed bifocals. Worse yet, I had to begin periodically saying "excuse me." I, who had been so correct all my life, never needing to utter that silly degrading phrase, now was making a habit of saying it, even to the likes of Babs and Peder.

Fortunately I seldom saw Adrian, let alone ran into him. Yes, Sabina not only forgave his temporary disappearance, but actually forgot all about it. Her intelligence though questionable seemed absolutely eclipsed by her uneasy passion for him. Personally, I find his overheated masculinity particularly gauche. She seemed like a character out of one of her absurd little mythological stories…some Greek shepherdess whisked away by some god. After the god had his way, something terrible always befell the hapless female. What happened to Sabina's bristly defiance? Just a few months ago, she would have smelled Adrian out immediately and proceeded to give him one her lectures on male oppression down through the ages. That is the trouble with mythology; there are so many messy, illogical metamorphoses. I cannot abide transformations. Fortunately my devotion to law enables me to maintain a steady course. I am at the helm of all changes. Generous person that I am, I frequently found myself drawn to Sabina's blowzy slightly smaller side of the office. Though she had betrayed me many a time, I felt some kind of sympathy for her. I would be there for her after her unfortunate though well deserved fall. Perhaps she would actually see the error of her ways. I would console her by allowing her back into my good graces.

As I walked by the partition of office and peeked in, she stuck out her hand in my general direction. "Julian, get a load of this." She was pacing the confines of her office. For a brief moment I actually felt some remorse that I had diminished the size of her walking track. In the flickering florescent light something sparkled on the ring finger of her right hand, as vulgar as Fourth of July fireworks.

"My dear, that's lovely. Did you buy it for yourself on the shopping channel?"

Even a month ago, the old Sabina would have bared her teeth, smiled, and said, "What would an old queen like you know about anything that was real?" Instead her smile deflated and her head drooped forward, her graying blond tresses fell over her eyes.

"Sometimes I just wish that he would call me more. I know he wants me to be his wife, but he disappears all the time, and when he's around I never know what he's thinking." She looked at me through her limp locks, desperate for some kind of succor.

I was disturbed. All change disturbs me. Allow one little thing to change and before you know it the whole world has become different and decidedly less comfortable. "Why Sabina when did you ever wait around for some man to talk to you? Is this your time of month, dear?"

"Julian I didn't mean it to be this way. I was simply listening to Babs read Latin poetry at The Empire, and every time I looked up this man was watching me with an intensity that I had never experienced before. I felt somehow that he knew me, and even worse that I knew him. Even stranger, he appeared to be understanding the Latin. When Babs switched to Greek, he hardly seemed to be able to contain his excitement. Gallantly he began translating it for me...it was a love poem. Then he walked back to his seat, but all the while I could feel his eyes on me, piercing through the smoke. I fled before Babs finished. I haven't run away from anything since the day a mad dog was loose on the farm when I was eight."

I kept my composure, trying to look attentive; she seemed to be in some kind of unfortunate state. Though I try not to suffer fools, and certainly she was acting like one, I knew she needed something from me.

She kept on. "Part of me was completely terrified; those burning eyes that always seemed to follow me, but I couldn't stop hearing the sound of his voice uttering that love poem with such overwhelming passion. I thought he was reciting it for me alone. When I was driving home, I actually had to pull over and park for a few moments. I seemed to have lost track of time and the road seemed to be writhing and twisting like a snake."

For one foolish moment, I wanted to share with her the recent distortions in my life, but then I thought better of it. After all I have my reputation to maintain, and she IS a junior colleague. I gave her a little pat on her stocky shoulder.

Her hands pressed against her face, and her whole body

seemed to shudder in some futile resistance. "I came back to hear Babs that next week. I knew I shouldn't, but it didn't matter what I knew; when Wednesday came around, I found myself driving to The Empire. I hated him; I didn't want to see him. I was only going to hear Babs recite her epic about the tragic destruction of the Goddess religions. Men, just because they know how to play power games, think they're better than women. I hate it. I don't even date. That mysterious man smelled of power. I sat down and promised myself that I would only look at Babs. I heard someone sit in the chair next to me...my body knew it was HIM. I felt his sweet, warm breath at my ear. He whispered to me. "I have been thinking about you all week. Don't run away again, I need you." I felt his hand rest on my shoulder, and I nodded.

She looked like a child pleading in need; as if somehow I could help her. I, the master of resourcefulness, did not know what to do. I could not let her know that I was frightened about what was happening around me, so I simply nodded my head.

No help in sight, she closed her eyes. Even I closed my eyes and bowed my head. That powerless moment seemed to stretch forever.

The campus bells tolled. When I opened my eyes Sabina was once again studying her ring sparkling in the florescent light. The sparkle had captured her once more. "He really is wonderful; that stone is magnificent. You know Julian, Adrian has a whole string of those coffee shops. He's going to go national soon. He'll have a whole empire, and I'll be its queen!"

I wanted her to stop. Even for Sabina this was far fetched. "But my dear he is so young, hardly twenty. I know men are supposed to be at their sexual peak at that age; but my dear what would you talk about? Or even worse what will you do when he spots a fresh young thing who of course thinks he's some sort of a hero. Just remember poor Ariadne." In my generosity I even stooped to note this tawdry mythological absurdity.

"Do I look all right Julian? I still look young, don't I? Just the other day someone said that I really didn't look thirty eight. I know my hair is turning gray, but I can start dying it. Do I look all right Julian? Everyone says how young I look."

I knew I needed to say something; the poor girl would work herself into a state. I wanted to help, I really did. "Why don't you go see Tony? He's an expert on trying to stay young. A little dye, a little cream, why he will help you look positively nubile."

I must have said something wrong. A frown tightened on her face and she squared her shoulders. "I'm not talking to Tony any more, after what happened at the party. You saw him, he tried to get Adrian's attention. As if anyone in their right mind could ever be attracted to that old queen!"

I was just about to remind Sabina that I had a not altogether academic interest in that old queen, when I saw tears welling up in her eyes, and I knew that this wasn't a time for the truth. For a moment I felt a wave of nostalgia for those days in which I could attempt to prod her back to the straight and narrow as she bristled defiantly. Then she rushed off, something to do with wedding.

I hate pretense, but I now was spending more and more time pretending that everything was continuing on its regular course. Not that on the surface, anything was really different for Tony and I. His family came over uninvited every Sunday. He cooked his Greek feast every Monday. He dropped his towel for me every morning. Some nights, he brushed his lips against various parts of my body, after which I stuck it to him. I tried not to think about that closed eyed moment of ecstasy that he once shared with me, and the strange dream I had after. This was not the time. And as far as those strange nightmares of his...chaos was seeping further into my orderly life...Tony stopped dying his hair and shaving his body. Gray fuzzy fur began springing up on his legs and chest.

Jerome seemed to take a particularly proprietary interest in me. Between trying to sell me bottles of seaweed extract, he would, apropos of nothing, tell me how much he admired my honesty, my scorn of mythology, and my absolute adherence to law. With his rictus of a smile, I could never tell if he was being serious or sarcastic. During one of those intimate tete a tetes he once confided in me how relieved he was that zealous Christians had ended the whimsical obscenity of the pagan world replacing it with a sober bureaucracy of power. "As far as the opposition, we know what to do with them, don't we Julian?" He made a poking jab with his arm.

Perhaps he was going a little bit too far, but I must admit that I admired Jerome's values. If only the Catholic Church would get rid of those ridiculous statues. Though no one takes them seriously, they are still too similar to the gods and goddesses that litter museums throughout the world corrupting impressionable minds. Just look at Sabina. Dare I say that I experienced a certain rapport with Jerome?

Cleo too became even more brazen, taking increasing liberties. Sitting next to me during one of our ritual breakfasts, I heard her slowly scooting her chair closer and closer to me. The smell of warm musk was overpowering. I felt her hand rest on my inner thigh as I slipped a forkful of babganoosh in my mouth. She blew into my ear and whispered, "Julian my firm love, soon you'll be left all to me."

Her hands were just beginning to tap Morse Code on my expanding member, when Mother interrupted that dauntless exploration. "Now Cleo, that's enough. That poor man is going to choke on his egg plant. You may have memorized the rhyme my children, but you've yet to learn the rhythm." Again there was a wrinkle in time she sat their motionless and silent, listening. Then she began singing some childish doggerel about rowing a boat down a stream, looking for some kind of response from us. Finally she opened her arms to the entire assemblage, even me. In her enthusiasm she knocked over the bottle of retsina, which gave me an opportunity to push out from the table. I held my napkin over my lap and grabbed a towel from the rack near the sink. This marked the end of another breakfast; the three began their exodus. When I turned to place the towel back on the rack, I felt a soft oily hand brush my backside and whisper passionately, "Soon."

CHAPTER 22

Julian walks hesitantly through the halls of the History department. He looks strangely vulnerable. Up ahead friendly laughter is coming from the faculty lounge just up ahead. His steps speed up until he stops, standing in the doorway expectantly.

Peder, Agnes and three other faculty are talking with non-stop playfulness as they sit around a table littered with coffee cups and bag lunches.

Julian watches hope fully.

Agnes notices him. She becomes silent. As the others look at her, she nods toward Julian sarcastically. All the diners are silent now as they stare at him.

Julian tries to smile.

No reaction from the others.

Julian adopts his usual look of cold superiority, turning away abruptly.

Agnes smirks, "EXCUSE ME."

Peder starts laughing. "Who died and left him in charge?"Julian flees as the diners' laughter echoes maliciously down the hallway.

Like a marionette, Julian marches on, straightening his tie and nodding mechanically. The campus bells start tolling.

Back in his office, pieces of white cloth are draped haphazardly over every available surface. The sound of scissors cutting fabric comes from Sabina's side of the partition.

Julian looking shocked at the chaos in his once orderly office, slams down his briefcase.

Sabina's voice nonchalantly comes from the other side of the partition. "Have you noticed that the bells have started ringing at such odd times. It's like someone put a spell on them."

Julian's anger evaporates. He pauses, "Yes, it's, it's very strange." He suddenly looks more human.

She peeks over the partition. "You look like you just saw a ghost." The bells stop tolling. "What did you say?"

"Oh nothing."

She darts into Julian's side of the room, holding up a white garment. "What do you think about this length for a toga?"

Julian studies it with his usual hauteur. "My dear, that's a lovely length. Who is it for, or does once size fit all?"

Teasingly she drapes the toga over Julian. "Why it's for you darling…for the wedding. The whole department is dying to see your legs."

He smiles in mock horror. Are YOU going to wear a tunic? You really should. That flowing robe hides a myriad of figure flaws. At least that's what Roman maidens thought."

All her teasing bravado disintegrates. She looks like a bewildered child. "I know it seems foolish but…"

Powerful footsteps are approaching in the hallway. Sabina's face is transformed into a look of radiant excitement.

Adrian, in all his young male splendor, enters the office.

Aside from his usual black vest with no shirt, he's wearing jean cutoffs and his feet are shod in sandals. "Salve Sabina!"

Sabina answers demurely, "Salve Hadrianus."

Julian stares at Sabina. "How dare you use that name?"

Adrian ignores the question, condescendingly glancing at Julian. "salve Julianus.!"

At the sound of that name, Julian looks startled, then frightened. He nods submissively.

Adrian examines the toga in Sabina's hand, then he drops the toga into Sabina's hands. "Watch the hem."

CHAPTER 23

Not that I could talk about any of this with Tony...after all I have my standards. I would not want to give the impression to him or anyone that I actually entertained an interest in the folly of his family, or even worse that that they knew something, that I with my critical intelligence did not understand. I have lived an uprighteous, solitary existence with my inside track to the infallible truth which reveals itself to those of us who are scrupulously rational. While people were deluding themselves with gods and goddesses frolicking in the fields of Greece, Plato was discovering the real world of universal truths shining unchangingly. Most people settled for mere shadows, but I, I look directly to the essential light, suffering fools benignly. But why do I look forward to those Sunday breakfasts?

That Monday night when I was pressing my fork through the fragile, crisp crust of spanikapita, I thought that I would admonish Tony, for the apparent neglect of his one time conspirator, Sabina. "After all Tony, she really is going through a hard time; I saw tears on her cheeks... absolutely incongruous, like seeing an Amazon cry. You must have a talk with her, you know about things like this.

I said that you could give her some tips on style; you are good after all at creating the illusion of beauty. You certainly spend an inordinate amount of time in that endeavor. By the way, what is with this new hirsuteness, and my dear what happened to that boyish black hair of yours? Is there some little impasse out of which I can guide you? After all what is a friend for if he cannot make little troubles disappear? I AM inordinately fond of you."

One of those crisp little pastry flakes appeared to have lodged in Tony's throat. Though his powers of swallowing, shall we say, recreational objects is almost legendary; it seemed as if a morsel of the spanikapita, despite his expertise had lodged in his throat. I was very patient. I did cover my plate with my napkin, just in case. He must have coughed for a good two minutes. When he finished, the poor dear had tears in his eyes, like some puppy with a cold. I felt some immediate stirring in my loins, but I knew that any interruption of my schedule would be unseemly. Though there was a certain poignancy to his tears, its origin was clearly gastronomic. I did pass my napkin over to him.

For a moment, and I hate to admit it, I witnessed a strange metamorphosis. Right before my eyes Tony seems to be changing shape in some absurd way. One minute he seemed a spoiled starlet who had just had a peevish fight with her boyfriend; and the next, with his gray hair and bristly face he looked almost more heroic, like a person caught face to face with some implacable and over powering foe, a Laocoman of a face watching the serpent devour his children and himself…where are these images coming from?

Then I noticed a little piece of pastry lodged on his nose. My preposterous reflections were dispelled. I bent over to him and brushed off his nose: the crumb took up residence on his chin. I did not mention anything about that of course. I just allowed that crumb to be there. My world was beginning to become so distorted, I didn't really know how to make things right. I was losing my edge, but I needed to reestablish my bearings.

I waited for an appropriate amount of time to press my point about Sabina. "Why Tony I thought you and Sabina were such familiar little companions, sharing all sorts of secrets behind my back. You must not be a fair weather friend now; unless of course there is something that I do not know about. Is there anything you need to make a clear breast of my boy? There are no little secrets are there? By the way what was that young brute that Sabina is unfortunately going to marry doing on his hands and knees in front of you that evening? After all from what I heard of your history, you would be the one more likely to be on your knees." I was trying valiantly to be sensitive; sensitivity is one of my trademarks.

The poor dear threw his napkin down on the table without as much as a thank you. "Julian, can't you see how hard I'm trying? Can't you for once get out of that stuffy little mind of yours and see me. I'm not a boy, I'm a man, an old man. In the ancient world I would probably be dead by now, and so would you! Wake up Julian."

Why the affront was almost too much for me. Tony may be an old man, but I, I am at the peak of my power. Why I can do as many push ups as I could when I was forty; and as far as waking up...this was suggested by a person whose vanity and foolishness rendered him almost comatose. Firmly I set him back on track. "Now Tony, if you are going to be that way about it, raising your voice so vulgarly, I will simply end this conversation right now, and leave you drowning in the predicament you call your life. By the way, can you pick out a present for Sabina and that brute, Adrian? They're getting married soon…nothing too expensive."

My announcement of the upcoming nuptials seemed to have shocked him out of his petty vindictiveness; he became so pallid that those puffy circles under his eyes looked even darker. He glared at me with something like determination. "He can't do that. He can't do that again!"

Perhaps the poor dear did have some misguided delusions about Adrian's attentions to him. Tony rubbed his eyes with the palms of his hands for a few moments and then nodded with what seemed like resignation. We were back to normal. He pouted at me and said, "This is a new brand of filo dough, Julian, the other had a kind of a greasy after taste." He poked at the last remaining flake on his plate and stuck it on his tongue. "Yes this is so much better, isn't it?"

The powers of reason were once more aligned. "Yes my dear, so much better."

That Monday night we had our usual little diversion, but this time when his mouth played against my lips and nipples and cock, there was not the customary response on my part. His mouth seemed desperate and greedy as if he wanted to draw something out of me. I have always hated desperation; it is so messy and unpredictable. People do things that they later regret. His sexual art was much too urgent that night.

He tried all his tricks, circumscribing the fleshy cap of my member with a flicking tongue. His sucking mouth grasped at the floppy noodle, pulling me with his clenched lips in a tug of war that left my reluctant penis caught in the middle. He even tried nibbling little bites that on other Monday evenings would have driven my cock to pounding pleasure. The poor old dear just did not have the knack that night…old, as if I were old.

Finally he simply stopped; I did not rub his inadequacies into his face though. As he turned away from me that night, I patted him on the shoulder as a sort of consolation prize. After all he had certainly tried. "You will pick up that present won't you, my dear. It would mean so much to Sabina, after all you were friends once; it is the least you can do."

"Yes Julian."

And did I already mention that Sabina and I were getting along famously? Someone needed to prod her back to normalcy. She had placed a rather large portrait of Adrian on her desk; he had one of those testosterone, alpha male smiles on his face. That portrait stood smack in front of the now forlorn pot bellied goddess. Funny how I have grown more fond of that fat little lady. Yesterday when I stopped by Sabina's office, I picked it up, brushed the dust off, and placed it a few inches further away from that macho portrait. Somehow she seemed more comfortable there.

Did I mention that Adrian and Sabina (mostly Adrian) had cooked up a ridiculous scheme to have a Roman wedding? Benignly I could only mutter (when did I start muttering instead of declaring?), "Young people these days..." He had probably been drinking beer and scratching his groin late at night and happened to see Spartacus on television. Or am I giving him too much credit? Probably he was simply looking for an excuse to expose his overdeveloped chest to a captive audience.

To get back to the topic of Sabina, the word "young" seems to have distressed her. She started to tear up.

To cheer her up I said, "Why what a positively original idea Sabina! He certainly is a clever boy. How interesting it will be for all of us to watch you play act."

But instead of delightfully going for my jugular, the messy dampness in her eyes began draining down her cheeks.

"Oh Julian, does he really think I'm old. I'm trying so hard. I bought one of those exercycles, don't you think my waist looks more trim, almost maidenly?"

"Better than maidenly my dear, you look positively regal."

Far be it from me to tell Sabina what she should be doing, but what was she doing…really? I had watched her claw her way up to this academic pinnacle where she was actually my junior peer, not my equal of course, and now she was about to give it up for this grandiose male on steroids. Maybe steroid induced impotency was the source of what Sabina calls his noble sexual restraint. "But what about all your little gods and goddesses, my dear? Who, but someone with your imagination, could bring them to life for all your eager students? What would this department be without you?" I dare say I spread my compliments on a bit thick, but it was appropriate for someone like Sabina, already numbed by mythological hyperbole.

"Julian, last night I woke up in a panic. I have been doing that more lately. I heard my heart pumping in my ears, and my whole body is drenched in sweat, and I knew, I just knew that that I am forgetting something dreadfully important. I racked my brain to try to remember. I started coming up with jumbled Latin words and images that didn't make sense to me. Just when I was about to understand what was going on, my mind became a blank video screen, and I felt so lost, so lost. And then when I remembered Adrian, so masterful and sure of himself, I knew that whatever I have forgotten wasn't really important."

I could tell she was long past reason. Someone had to step in, and I was responsible for having introducing her to the ancient world. If only she had listened to my advice and not begun her dangerous dabbling into primitive mysteries.

But now the deed was done. "All fine and good Sabina, but promise me that you will not hand in your resignation before talking with me first."

She looked at me blankly as if she could not understand why anyone would be so concerned about something so inconsequential.

"Now my dear Sabina, promise me right now that you won't do anything foolish without consulting with me. That's what friends are for. Promise me now on the belly of your fat little goddess." I placed my hand on the bulbous protruding stomach of that forlorn deity.

Sabina smiled with a hint of her former shark like eagerness. "She's a beauty isn't she?"

Beauty is not exactly the word I would use, but I nodded in hopes of stimulating an acquiescence to my request.

"Okay Julian, you've got your way. I won't do anything drastic about this stupid job until I talk with you first."

CHAPTER 24

Tony stands naked in the dingy bathroom. Motionless, he is looking somewhere in the distance, gazed unfocused. The last of the afternoon sun casts a golden glow on his gray-haired body.

A siren sounding in the distance wakes him to the moment. He stares into the small mirror that hangs above the sink. His haunted eyes fix on the image there.

A young and breath-taking beautiful Tony stares back at him.

CHAPTER 25

Normally I sleep the deep sleep of the just, even with my one nightly trip to the bathroom (I can assure you that that extra little trip to the bathroom has nothing to do with old age. I simply am very conscientious about drinking enough fluids in the course of my day).

Now, even my bastion of sleep was being disturbed by Tony. He seemed to spend the entire night tossing and muttering things in his sleep. I would wake up several times a night; he would be lying on his back, his hands extended toward the ceiling pleading for something. His normally seductive tone of voice was gone; he appeared to be presenting a case as if to some person or jury. He sounded desperate, mustering all his intelligence and will. Try as I would (not that I was spying), I could never make any sense out of his exclamations. They seemed like a veritable a stew of languages. I had no idea that Tony had received an education in the classics...I am sure that I picked out Roman and Greek words in his mutterings. I could make out a kind of rhythm to his voice, but I could never make out a meaning, and he sounded heartrendingly young.

Finally I would open my eyes and turn over to look at

the source of this youthful pleading, and there lying next to me was gray bearded Tony. Each night he would plead his case in that broken medley of languages, and then after what most certainly must have been the defeat of his cause, he would stop breathing, all the while tremors shaking his body. Finally silence and stillness would engulf him, and once again he would sleep, but not a serene sleep. He would lay, hardly breathing, his skin drained of any color. One night I even touched him just to make sure he was alive. He felt cool and damp...his body stirred, but not from some inner spark of wakefulness. It seemed that something from the outside was attempting to jerk him out of his stupor only to once again release him, dumping him back, livid onto my bed.

I have never really been afraid before. After all laws are immutable and I am an upright man. But every night now listening to the music of that desperate pleading and then turning to see the corpse of an old man next to me, I began being afraid of the dark for the first time in my memory. I'd lie awake feeling a chill permeate the bed. The moon would look in the window, not casting light, but only an unearthly glow, a fluorescence that would unhitch my imagination and let it run wild.

Several times a night, he would suddenly gasp as if he were drowning, and then with a sigh of despair, release that tortured air into the bedroom. I thought I could smell putrefaction. Yet when I woke to light of morning, I, Julian Scribner, who never wasted a moment in embarrassment, felt ashamed of my terror. How could I ever be frightened of something in the night; let alone if it had to do with the foolish old man next to me? Sitting at my desk in the morning, I could hardly believe that I had come to this. I increased the number of my push ups. Every day in every way,

I'm getting better. I added another frozen banana protein drink to my late afternoon regimen on Saturdays when I seem particularly vulnerable. Just because Tony is letting himself rot away, there is no need for me to give up. Yes, every day in every way I am getting better.

Of course I could not talk to anybody about this, especially Tony. I have my reputation to maintain. Being afraid...that is for foolish people. Besides how could I tell anyone, that each night I feel like I was in bed with a corpse?

But then I had a kind of revelation that provided a temporary relief...Tony had a problem. I love concrete problems, something I can work on and always eventually surmount. The revelation took place at one of our, shall I say, Sunday family breakfasts. It is the one time of my week that I do not have to pretend that everything is normal. I can take comfort in the general craziness that after all is not mine. In fact all that absurdity around me makes anything that I can imagine seem tame and by contrast...almost ordinary.

Once again that Sunday I took my customary place among that eccentric menagerie. I saw myself as an outsider who had an academic interest in all their folly. Listless Tony was sitting next to his glamorous and fragrant sister. She looked over at him, and in a voice loud enough to catch everyone's attention announced. "Why Tony are you having some kind of hygiene difficulty? You smell stronger than your goat cheese. I thought gods were beyond that kind of thing."

Jerome nudged me with his sharp little elbow and cackled in satisfaction. "See! The beautiful Tony is human after all. Original sin is a chancre festering and growing in all humanity. Only the salvific and efficacious blood of Christ or Maine grown wheat grass can save us."

Cleo turned to me, winked, and then addressed her disheveled brother again. "Why Tony, you'd thing you were afraid of water. What you need is a nice long bath, to feel yourself surrounded and engulfed by water. Wouldn't that be delightful? And poor Julian here wouldn't have to deal with that dead goat smell."

You have no idea how relieved I was to know that what I was smelling at night did not originate in some overheated fantasy...the smell was real, so real that other people noticed it too. I was beginning to have a grudging respect for Tony's siblings.

I had been having difficulty even looking at Tony; even during the day he reminded me of my nightmares. But now prodded by the concern of his brother and sister, I knew that I needed to examine him more closely. The sight surprised me, even dare I say, touched me. His hair, no longer in hyacinthine curls, lay in knotted masses of gray untended on his head. His beard looked musty and yellowish. His face was pale and puffy as if those nightly bouts of his were draining him of his last bits of vitality, and the smell, there was definitely a smell.

Wonderful, wonderful, my senses were not lying. What was happening was simply a break of decorum, an interruption of hygiene, something that could be solved with a few kind but firm words. I rose to the occasion, for Tony's sake. "Why Tony you look positively a wild man. Your family deserves more than this from you. After all when you serve food to guests, it is imperative that you, like the food be fresh!"

He sat among us, his head hanging down. Without even glancing in my direction he looked at his mother as if she might be a final source of solace. "I'm trying so hard, I really am. I can't stand the feeling of water. Even doing dishes drives me mad. I know this time I'm supposed to do something different, but I just don't know how. The rhyme keeps repeating, no matter how hard I try. This time around I wanted to be able to lead an ordinary life and grow old, with an ordinary man, so ordinary that he's foolish...and now it's happening again. All the players are appearing. How can I stop it?"

I had thought or at least hoped that despite Tony's evident foolishness he had been spared the strain of madness that ran through his family...alas.

Mother's eyes silently rested on Tony. They looked at each other; the moment stretched on in silence. Then the omelet which had been drenched in olive oil and garlic took its toll on Mother's stomach. She released a loud garlic flavored belch.

I was shocked that a mother would set such a vulgar example for her children, but this was not the time to set Mother straight.

In fact she seemed almost proud of her performance and smiled blissfully at me as if she had just demonstrated some grotesque lesson for my benefit. Then she actually addressed me, "Feel it bubble up and out. Let go, let go into the abyss." Needless to say no Scribner, let alone my dear mother, would make such a spectacle of herself let alone use such toilet language at the table. Then with appetite undiminished she dug back into her omelet with lip smacking gusto. She began humming that absurd ditty about rowing a boat up a stream...such foolishness!

Of all the absurd suggestions! At that moment I had serious doubts about the moral fiber of Mother. Was she one of those reckless welfare mothers? Even more scandalous... were several men involved in the fatherings? I really care about Tony. He may have lost his knack for inciting my pleasure and he may have some dilemma around hygiene, but these problems are not insurmountable. I decided that it was my duty to role model parenting skills to Mother. "Why Tony, your with me now, and you have the support of a loving family. Whatever is happening...a stiff upper lip and maybe a few trips to a therapist, why, we can be back to normal. Now I think you ought to start today with a new resolve. Simply step into that shower; there is nothing of which you need be afraid. Are you a man or a mouse?"

Then I had a brilliant idea (I would have made a wonderful parent!). "Why don't you go right now Tony. We will all just sit here at the table and wait for you to shower. Won't we? We all care about you. You can do it. Come on!"

Jerome had a self satisfied look on his face, and Cleo began tracing circles on my inner thigh. A delicate almost imperceptible veil of sorrow fell over Mother's face. It must be difficult for a mother to recognize how little she knows about parenting. I realized with characteristic compassion that incompetence and not immorality was at the root of the poor old dear's lack of skills. I was just about to suggest a book on the subject to her, when I was rudely interrupted.

"Now Julian, STOP IT, STOP IT RIGHT NOW! You don't know what you are asking of me. You don't know what you're saying." Tony was all fluffed up in hysteria.

I was careful to maintain my parental dignity. "If you're going to be that way about it..."

"That's it, Julian old boy. You show him." Jerome was clapping his hands in righteous delight.

Spurred on, I looked at Tony; I was preparing to lay down strict but fair consequences for his insolence. What I saw startled me. He no longer looked upset; a kind of sadness replaced his stubborn defiance. His eyes dampened and he made one quiet little sniffing sound. Then he looked straight into my eyes; for some bizarre reason it felt like he was saying goodbye. There was certainly no need for that.

Despite all my resolve, I found myself moved...I remained silent.

Tony spoke with restraint, "Now the breakfast is over. It's time for everybody to leave. We need to get on with it." He stood up quietly and walked up the stairs to the room that I use for storing old magazines.

For all my good intentions something seemed to have broken in Tony that day. He never did dishes after that. By the next Sunday breakfast the sink was piled high. As if by some mysterious premonition, Jerome brought Chinese take out and paper plates. He also wore some sort of faintly oriental robe and was selling of incense.

Even more interesting, that night after his acting out behavior, Tony moved into the spare bedroom. My sleeping pattern returned almost to normal, but some nights I would wake up and just have to peek into his room to ascertain if he was still breathing. Despite the smell and stubbornness, he is after all my very dear man.

CHAPTER 26

J ulian sits dreamily at his desk, eyes out of focus, gazing out
the window. A breeze, something which he always avoids
especially in his office, gently whispers through the screen.
The sound of playing children, high voices full excitement,
filters through; he smiles ever so slightly.

A blue late summer sky, the sun softening, nostalgic…
is that sadness flickering across Julian's face? A few yellow
leaves flutter down.

Tony, looking a mess, slowly walks down the wooden
stairs. He seems in a trance.

Julian looks up, his wistfulness is replaced by confusion.
The two make eye contact and hold it for a few dizzy
moments.

A dog howls in the distance.

Tony looks away.

Julian composes himself. "It's that foolish wedding
Saturday…masquerading as Romans…fraternity freshmen.
It is beyond ridiculous.

Tony stands motionless with his head down.

Julian tries to smile reassuringly, but his eyes look
frightened. "I wouldn't go myself to that travesty, but she's

my junior colleague…I thought I should mention it to you. But you don't need to go…really."

Tony looks up, gently.

Through the open window, Mother approaches along the sidewalk, pushing her cart, the wheels squeaking.

Tony solemnly walks to the door as it opens.

Julian watches, and then stands up too.

Mother pushes her cart up to the front steps of the house and rummages through the pile of junk that she pushes along. She spots something near the bottom and gently pulls it up through the rustling contents. She examines it closely and then with some satisfaction lifts it toward Tony: folded cloth, simple and homespun.

He watches her.

They make eye contact. She softly nods.

Tony walks down the steps and receives his gift, his hands shaking.

Julian peeks out the door, looking aghast at the pile of junk in his yard.

Mother turns her attention to him. "You've got yours all ready."

Julian's confusion is turning into irritation.

She cautions him. "Don't forget about the omelet."

She turns away and pushes her cart humming her childhood rhyming ditty.

CHAPTER 27

Usually I love the corridors of the history department in summer. Not that I have any sort of romance with summer (I have always believed that it is absolutely essential to have a stoic attitude about the seasons. After all they are simply demonstrations of higher laws...the tilt of the earth and the complicated but mechanical effect this has on the jet stream; only puny minds get preoccupied by the daily weather), but to get back to the corridors of the history department: they are so lovely and empty in the summer, like a serene mausoleum. The few professors that I happen upon are only there to briefly and belatedly tidy their offices. It is true that there are a few devoted souls like myself whose intellectual frontiers expand during summer, but they are as tactfully retiring as I...no annoying little birthday parties or even worse, rambunctious lunches where my fellow professors giggle and describe in gruesome detail what they ate the night before.

The entrée for those unsavory meals in the faculty lounge is of course departmental politics. How faculty love to find a cause, no matter how petty. I have learned to rise above this vulgar behavior and eat my chaste lunch in my office.

When I do make a very occasional foray into that lounge (I am a team player you know), I make sure to guide the conversation to sober, historical topics. My fellow professors always listen in quiet respect. My serious intellectual tour de forces set an inspiring example for them all. The clarion call of my discourse inevitably reminds them that they too have serious intellectual pursuits...one at a time they all excuse themselves to explore those pressing academic concerns. I am, indeed a role model.

The final blissful touch to those summer halls is the fact that they are not filled with lolling students eagerly vying for the attention of professors. It is true that a few students wander through the halls, but they are usually more formally dressed and older...serious students, summer school students, who are wise enough to know that though the rest of the world frolics, they have more important things to do...my kind of student.

Unfortunately that was a different sort of summer. Sabina was getting married Saturday; try as I would to gently dissuade her. She was continuing to use her office (really our office) as a costuming factory for that faux Latin event. The fore mentioned whole office was strewn with yards and yards of white fabric on which she was snipping and sewing like a busy little beaver. She even rented a sewing machine, pushing her desk aside...not a good omen. At first I wondered why she chose to do all that busy little work at the office, then I noticed how she kept popping over to my side of the partition as if what I was doing was certainly less important than her circus of a wedding. I even wondered at times if by annoying me, she was really trying to get my attention, as if I was supposed to stop her.

"Julian what do you think about this length for a tunic?

Do you think that my hair is thick enough to braid flowers in it?"

Now normally I pride myself on my masculine and marine like composure, not over done off course; because I also exhibit a paradoxically deep sensitivity to human need. With characteristic insight I realized that poor dear Sabina was afraid. Who wouldn't be, on the verge of being married to that barely dressed testosterone boy? "My dear, your hair is a bit wispy, but in all the foolishness of the wedding no one will notice."

She kept giving me glimpses of that tawdry relationship of her. "Adrian may not be very expressive, but I can tell he's really excited about this event. He's constantly making trips to the library checking all the Latin texts. Why just yesterday, he corrected me on of my Latin. That's all we speak when we are alone. He says he loves to hear me speak Latin, even though I don't do it very well. He has decided that I need to learn Greek next. Doesn't that mean he loves me Julian? For what other reason would a young man take all that effort to guide me?"

I was just getting ready to remind her about the eccentricities of young male behavior (just look at the way they wear their hats backwards; sometimes when I pass them in the hallways I want to slap them and turn their hats to the proper position...I am not going to even mention how they wear their pants). I was just about to say, "What's so impressive about a little parroted Latin," when the very object of this controversy walked into the office. He was wearing his usual black vest to enhance the kind of sweating, naive majesty that young males manage so well.

"Salve Sabina."

"Salve Hadrianus."

He positioned himself in the very center of the room

and just stood there in all his hormonal splendor. Aside from his usual black vest, he wore an abbreviated pair of shorts under which his muscular legs bristled like a goat's. His feet were shod in what looked like imitation Roman sandals. He stood there clearly unaware of the inappropriateness of his casual state of undress, imperially surveying Sabina. If he were a student I would have certainly cut him down to size.

He condescendingly glanced over at me, "Salve Julianus."

I nodded coldly. There is no way this precocious child was going to make me play his pig Latin game, after all...

With absolute noblesse oblige he smiled at Sabina. "I see the togas are coming along...well done." Then he turned his whole body in my direction; he stared at me straight on with green eyes so intense that even I, the master of the intimidating stare, looked down. "I presume that you're coming to the wedding, Julianus."

I found myself nodding in silence.

Then he stretched his muscular arm out at me and pointed at a spot between my eyes. "Make sure your friend comes." Motionlessly he held that pose, I found myself backing against the wall still nodding. Normally I never nod; it signifies an unseemly acquiescence to someone else's power, but there I was...I could not stop my head from making that idiotic motion. He finally turned around and to no one in particular said, "Splendid." Then he was gone, leaving behind the sour smell of submission...this time it was my own scent.

"Isn't he wonderful Julian, so masterful, so appreciative! He likes my togas and tunics.

I suppose you have to bring Tony now. From what you've said about his current state we'll keep him way in back. Adrian loves beauty so, and I don't want to spoil it for him. I'm dying my hair black, Hadrian's crazy about black hair."

"My dear girl he certainly is something."

"He's wonderful and he's mine."

I could feel my armpits soaked in perspiration. I never sweat; even my body was becoming unreliable.

She returned to her determined sewing. For a moment I wanted to talk with her, to talk with anybody, about the way Tony looked at night, about that strange family of his, about that dream I had in which Adrian lifted his arms up toward the house, about the way Sabina's behavior did not make sense anymore, about the way I perspired when Adrian looked at me...

Without even pausing in her endeavors, she said, "You'll bring Tony won't you? When Adrian gets like that you just have to do what he wants." A hint of confusion passed over her face.

I was silent. I had spent the last two years trying to keep Tony out of my public life. Now the whole world, or at least Adrian, demanded that Tony come with me to this absurd masquerade. This time though, it was not so much that I was embarrassed about Tony's absurdity. Since everything in my life was gradually becoming preposterous, I did not care as much any more about keeping him hidden, and besides everyone had already seen him. I was concerned about something else. When I tried to focus on that feeling with my usual insightful precision, my mind would go in circles.

I just knew that I didn't want Tony to come to this travesty of a nuptial. It was not because he smelled either, that barnyard odor seemed almost like a friend, although a friend from whom I needed to keep some distance. I did not want Tony involved in this event; I had a vague feeling of dread...the way he kept saying to Mother, "I'm trying so hard, I'm trying so hard." What could he be talking about, and why couldn't he just let me fix it.

Sabina must have been reading my mind. She commanded, "Bring him!"

"Of course." I smiled as if giving my blessing. I could feel the weight of Adrian's shadow.

And on that day I almost did not mention it to Tony. Since he no longer seemed to be in contact with Sabina, I thought that the evening of the wedding (strangely it was a twilight wedding…how appropriate for this benighted event) I would simply slip out of the house as if I were going to the office…with my toga ready in my briefcase. I really didn't want to tell him. Lately those eyes of his looked so frightened, as if something terrible were about to happen. His gray bearded face looked so incongruous with those startled young eyes of his. I actually wished that we were still sleeping together; I could at least hold him and rock those terrified eyes closed for a few moments of peace. Indeed this gerrymandering world around me was dulling my edge.

CHAPTER 28

Hesitantly Julian walks up the stairs of his own house; he reaches into his briefcase searching for his keys, pauses, alarmed, and then shrugs hopelessly. The door is partially open. Once again he is able to muster a look of disapproval; to no one in particular he demands, "Tony! How many times do I have to tell you to keep the door locked? My priceless files…"

At first there is no answer; even the clocks are silent. The Julian hears movement upstairs and then the soft padding of bare feet.

Tony's bare feet are now visible as he walked down the stairs. Now his whole towel-draped body is in sight.

Julian gives a gasp of surprise. His look of disapproval melts away.

Tony's hair is once again hyacinthine black and his body as smooth as a boy's.

"I am glad that you finally started taking care of yourself. You have done wonders."

Tony barely glances in his direction.

"What is the occasion? Were you finally willing to take my supportive direction?"

Tony looks up at him in adolescent sadness. "You wanted me to do it, you wanted me to go to him. You said it was good for your career. I didn't matter to you."

For a second Julian looks bewildered and then his face tightens in characteristic disapproval. "What a foolish, foolish thing to say to me! I invited you in to my house to stay here despite your strange behavior. I am not even mentioning your family. What are you talking about?"

Tony keeps staring at him in calm reproach.

"This is absurd! I don't know what you are talking about." Julian pauses then begins looking concerned. "Just take some deep breathes, relax, you have been having a bad dream." He reaches out his hand toward Tony. "Just wake up, clear your mind, I'm right here."

Tony looks directly in Julian's eyes. "Who's having a dream?" Then he walks away.

CHAPTER 29

And I began having dreams on a regular basis. Previously, I slept the sleep of the just. On those rare occasions that I did dream, there was always a reason. That wretched dream about Adrian reaching toward my house was clearly an outcome of a late night, a full bladder, and most importantly, the repercussions of that wretched evening at Sabina's house surrounded by people who believed in the idiocy of mythology and its handmaiden, ritual. I was the victim of second hand myth. If I ever go to such a foolish event again I'll wear a respirator to protect my sober lungs.

Did I mention that I never leave anything unfinished? I believe that this had been the source of my serene, dreamless nights. The unfinished swill of other peoples' hopes and deeds laps back over them at night. My pristine life never needed that kind of backwash. At least that's how it used to be; then I began being plagued by a reoccurring dream... each night it would be the same. I would dream that I had woken up in a strange place; all around me was a darkness which no matter how hard my eyes strained, they couldn't pierce. Somehow I knew that I had to remain absolutely still; my life depended on it. That is when I would feel a very slight swaying motion as if the ground underneath me were not altogether dependable. I would be paralyzed in terror, yet somehow I knew that I needed to do something very important. Suddenly off in the distance, the edge of glowing red object peaked over the horizon. I watch it, entranced, as it gradually widened and bulged into an angry red face.

As I heard the sound of a dog howling, I realized that that face was the rising moon. Even stranger, I knew I was on a boat. Instead of feeling relief in my newly discovered orientation, I could feel a cold fist tighten and clench in my stomach. I couldn't take my eyes off the moon as it rose swollen from the horizon. The moon quietly silhouetted a crab like palm tree.

That's when each night I would hear the sound of something slip into the water. The swaying underneath me would increase into a slight rocking motion as the boat released its burden. Then a moment of no sound… as I watched the moon edge just a little higher. Just as the rocking was beginning to subside I would hear a brief gurgling agitation in the water followed by a slight splash, but I held my gaze on the moon with absolute despairing determination.

That's when I would hear a little clinking sound from somewhere on the boat…a meaningless random sound that seemed to let me know that whatever had been happening was now over. I cautiously lowered my eyes to what I now recognized as a river, to see one last ripple broadcast itself over the watery reflection of the moon. Then even the ripple disappeared. My stomach was no longer gripped in terror, but I felt no relief at the passing of danger, but rather a dull disappointment about something I had left cravenly undone. I knew some essential part of myself had rippled away in that reflection of the moon. I fled silently into the dark belly of that ship that carried me, knowing that I must not remember what I had experienced.

At that point I would wake up, as if the prospect of forgetting were an insurmountable problem, and that only waking could relieve the tension of that dilemma. I would find myself alone in my bed in Minneapolis, and though I would try to exchange the thoughts of my very important historical projects for that strange dream, somehow in the chill of the night, I knew that I had lost something that made all the papers and files of my life scatter into meaninglessness, and that the meaningless was taking on a form beyond my understanding. Some darker being, by reason of its great and hidden mass, was drawing my usual life into a configuration beyond my intelligence. Perhaps that was why I could not forget the dream; it seemed a messenger of doom.

Raving, I know it's all raving and you don't understand what I mean...I didn't understand either, but waking from that dream I would feel shocked and horrified. At that point, I would usually get up and walk to the next room to see if Tony was all right. I would watch him for minutes at a time; it was not passion or contempt, I simply wanted to know that he was there, safe.

Just two days before that wedding, the order of the universe took one last jolt. I was walking outside of Fordham hall, valiant as ever. Despite time stretching and roads twisting and even my infallibility eroding; I still felt a poignant nobility about myself, a last stand at the Alamo heroism. If I were to be blown away, at least it would be with me head unbowed.

The day was brilliant as I had walked across campus, summer exploding all around...the sweet sour smell of newly moan grass ached in my nose, two young men with shirts off and chests just beginning to become heavy were throwing a

Frisbee around. Each man would throw the projectile, and with a meditative gaze, watch it float up into the air, and then would whoop wildly as his companion caught it. A young woman walked by with a dog on a leash. The short-haired mutt had a white plastic cone around his head like a nun's wimple. Its tongue was lopsidedly hanging out of one side of his mouth as he panted rapidly. His eyes inside the funnel seemed to bounce around from one side of the prison to the other, as if his whole self, not simple his face was squeezed into that narrow tunnel.

"Julianus come over here."

The voice was clear and deep and spoke with such authority that I turned in its direction and began walking like a somnambulist. I looked up to see myself approaching Adrian surrounded by a troop of young collegians. I noticed how natural he looked in his usual state of undress and how he held the center of that group with a kind of imperial authority. His troops looked at him hungry for a role, no matter how insignificant, in whatever story he was telling. I found myself walking up to Adrian nodding with awe and submission.

He stopped spinning his tale and looked towards me... all the other eyes following his lead, focusing on me, not because of my own importance, but simply because HE had bestowed his gaze on me. Strangest of all though, I found myself being grateful for his attention. "Now Julianus tell Sabina that we'll be needing two more toga's, and I want you to make a copy of the *Edict Perpetuam* for me, and give it to Tony." He turned his attention back to his admirers and once again all eyes begged him for more. I bowed, submitting to his will.

That day, even as I felt revulsion at my own head bowing submission, I carefully completed the ordered tasks.

Although when I handed the *Edict* to Tony I didn't mention who asked me to give it to him.

On the morning of the wedding I got up as usual, as if this were just another ordinary Saturday. The wedding was scheduled in the evening. My calisthenics dutifully done, I made my frugal breakfast. I hoped to renew my sense of well being with that sweet and fishy tasting substance. As it slid down my throat and into my slightly reluctant stomach I could almost feel my world righting itself. Indeed I spent much of the day exploring the last days of Hadrian.

(Did I mention already that I had started to take an extra dose of my nutritious breakfast in the late afternoons on Saturdays? It gave me added support in my valiant resistance to chaos) that afternoon I took a banana out of the freezer (did I mention that when I started this nutritious regimen, I began buying over ripe, inexpensive bananas in bulk, and then would peel and freeze them. I would take one of those hard brown bananas and place it in the blender with all the other ingredients of my ambrosia). That afternoon with hope renewed, I placed it in the blender, turning it on. It sputtered for a moment, locked in apprehension. Finally something broke free and as the motor began purring reassuringly and those ingredients began churning into a brownish green mass; I knew I had another chance this day to keep my world on track. I drank it; yes, everyday, in every way, I am getting better and better.

My concoction tasted different that afternoon. In fact it tasted downright gamy and not nearly as sweet, although I try not to be a slave to anything as ephemeral as taste. I also realized that I must not have blended the mixture long enough because I kept picking little strands of what must have been sprouts from between my teeth. I even began wondering if my stock of frozen bananas had somehow gone off. I looked in the freezer, and there to my horror I noticed TWO bags with brown cigar shaped objects in them. One bag I had carefully labeled "bananas." The other almost identical bag was labeled in Tony's messy scribble "pork sausages, uncooked." How many times do I have to tell Tony that pork is almost as indigestible as human flesh? Just then an overpowering belch burst out of my stomach and into the room leaving a rancid raw pork taste in my mouth.

As my stomach heaved I knew that not only was that raw meat indigestible and filthy (who knows from what part of the garbage-eating pig the components of the sausage originated), but that I had probably ingested some horrid and infectious organism that would hatch and lodge in one of my organs growing into some great hook faced worm...I sat at my desk and tried to work. Try as I might the printed words blurred and wiggled before my eyes ever so much like that wormy organism already planning to take up permanent residence in my beleaguered body. For a moment all life seemed like corruption. Even worse, I couldn't find meaning in those ancient codices set before my eyes.

I sat in my chair; my stomach roiled in disgust. In moments of very temporary relief, I gazed out the window. The world seemed poignantly ordinary. The dry leaves of August whispered against each other in the breeze; I thought that I could smell the bittersweet fragrance of summer waning. I saw a flock of geese rise and swoop into a smooth spiral climbing up and into the sky. Maybe the leaves had whispered to them about the coming of winter on this late August afternoon on the day of the marriage. Just then another belch rose out of me, all rotten and anxious.

At 6:00 a.m., I snapped my briefcase shut. Tony stepped out of his room...no coy dance with his towel.

With an instinct as compelling as geese fleeing the cold,

words slipped out of my mouth. "Oh, by the way Tony, Sabina and Adrian are getting married this evening. Of all the scatterbrained sophomoric ideas, the bizarre nuptial is taking place on a boat in the river. I know how much you are concerned about the dangers of water. I'll be leaving in a few minutes. You don't have to go; I know you're not feeling well. I think it's going to be such a foolish event anyway."

There…my duty to Adrian was done. So strange…I wasn't going to say a word, not that I would actually hide something from Tony, or even worse, Adrian, but I was relieved that Tony was still in the bathroom when I left. I stepped in the car and sped away from the house that fortunately still held my troubled but temporarily safe friend. The sun hung low in the blue western sky, casting long shadows across the road; how wonderful to look forward to so many Saturdays ahead of me, Tony puttering around at home, endless volumes of ancient documents waiting for me to read. My stomach suddenly heaved; I tasted the sourness of fear in my throat…yes, I was going to that ridiculous charade. Snapping my briefcase open just to make sure that it contained my toga (I judiciously waited for a stop sign to perform that operation), I pulled out that venerable garment; how well I would look, as if I were born to it.

CHAPTER 30

Through the windshield the streets are writhing, Julian struggles to stay on the road. The digital clock on the dashboard is frozen at 12 midnight. He holds onto the steering wheel desperately studying his frightened ashen face in the rear view mirror. He whispers, "Every day in ever way…" His stomach convulses. "Christ!"

His face relaxes slightly. The streets begin to smooth out a little, and his rapid breathing slows down. He looks out at the familiar world of the campus; the late afternoon light makes the world seem golden. He drives into the parking lot, and stops the car. He straightens his tie straining to force his face into a facsimile of composure and steps out of the car.

The blue sky deepens, darkness subtly stealing in. Here and there a forlorn bird calls out from the over arching trees. A few students scurry across the Commons, heading home to prepare fro the revels of Saturday night. Julian glances at a squat temporary looking building at the far end of the Commons. Cars whir over the bridge right behind it. He pauses studying the bridge apprehensively, then slowly solemnly walks toward the building.

The sound of rustling clothes comes from a stall in the gray institutional bathroom. The stall door slowly opens revealing a haunted greenish looking Julian dressed in a Roman toga. He walks uncertainly as his stomach rumbles. He struggles over to a sink with a mirror over it. His hands grip the sink; slowly and grimly lifting his head to see his reflection.

In the mirror stands an image; it looks a few years younger than Julian, but has an expression of icy composure. In dream like slow motion it studies shaky Julian with patronizing contempt.

Julian looks ashamed.

The image shakes its head in disapproval.

Julian's eyes are drawn and fixed to that contemptuous image; his face slowly transforms; now he is the reflection.

The image speaks. "How I hate trips, the thought of being on the wild sea or any body of water in fact turns my stomach queasy, not that I ever share my abhorrence with the magnificent Hadrianus. I am after all, Julianus, a mere secretary, humble and useless, a plebian, a bit player. All of us, or at least anyone who flourishes for any length time in his court, is aware that we must never create the impression that somehow our illustrious ruler needs us or even worse owes us a debt of gratitude for some task well done. I am the humblest of his servants, and I know how the land lies (how I love to keep a good secret). The provinces are littered with people who have successfully performed tasks for Hadrianus only to receive a sentence of exile.

Our great Hadrianus does not like to be reminded of his needs, let alone debts. I play the fool; not taking on the role of jester exactly; even that has hidden dangers. After all if the jester becomes too necessary for imperial distraction, the poor fool will soon find himself exiled to some dismal place like Dacia. Hadrianus' generosity shines on people who make foolish blunders, and I am the perfect master of foolish mistake.

I am the ever incompetent secretary who relies on Hadrianus' mercy for further employment. Hadrianus loves to be merciful. He talks with gardeners, cooks, and livery boys; he is famous for his common touch, a touch that lets the world know how utterly uncommon he is. Indeed he is loved by those far beneath him with whom he makes occasional contact, but feared by those who come close enough to have any prolonged usefulness. I understand the game. In the provinces it has been whispered that I have made an art of dissembling servility, but I see myself as a stoic who has adapted to the reality of the world of Hadrianus. My papers are my true witness, all the notes, all the laws that I have written in our dear emperor's name.

Perhaps I had succeeded too well; I during those last years, when he roamed the vacant corridors of his villa begging to die. But I am getting ahead of myself. Perhaps his fate had been cast long before by the vindictive stars, during that last trip of his that ended in the fiasco on the Nile...I should have seen that something was amiss, and shall we say, bailed out. Up until that point Hadrianus had succeeded in training us to believe in his invincibility.

What was to be a triumphant procession through his empire became some sputtering low comedy ending in a failure not worthy of the name tragedy. After all in tragedy a person recognizes some painful fate and suffers...of course I'm sure that whatever happened to that tragic hero was his own fault...really. Hadrianus disdained anything as ordinary as human fate. He survived by being splendid, the one beyond compare. In those last years even his agony was beyond the reach of human sympathy, although sympathy has never been my strong suite.

Yes that last outing of his was far different from his usual triumph. I suppose that was when the others began noticing that his carefully constructed world was coming apart. I stuck with him to the end, too busy plying the winds of his favor to notice that it really did not matter any more. Despite all the laws I helped him to write (not that I took any credit for that), the world he created began unraveling. By the end, he was the only person in the empire who did not know his glorious dream was over. All that time I lived under his spell or perhaps, dare I say, he lived under mine. Who would have thought that the world of marble and gold that Hadrianus built around himself would be his tomb.

Some people blame it on the boy of course. After all what is a grown up Caesar doing parading around his empire with a beautiful boy in tow. Certainly his predecessor the glorious Trajan plowed through a series of beautiful young males without so much as a hint of gossip. Men will be men you know. Whether it's a pair of young female breasts or the luscious orbs of a boy's buttocks, they all invite a man of power, especially an emperor.

But our dear grandiose Hadrianus attempted to make a penchant into something very Greek and heroic. He was to be the powerful hero who imparted his wisdom and an incidentally his semen. This would be as close as he would come to needing another person, but even then, it was for the sake of the young hero and posterity. How else could a childless emperor pass on the seed of his magnificence? He went through a series of those boy wonders. Of course each would only last for a few months. So many boys, so little time. Still, to Hadrianus this next young man was always to be the true and ultimate paragon of young maleness.

Our dear Hadrianus had such a vivid and forceful imagination. To hear him talk of his protégés was a thing of wonder. He could turn a squalid arrangement into a heroic scenario; painting a noble picture, touched up and renewed with each successive boy.

After all each boy was a hero in the making, rising at dawn, washing sleep from eager juvenile eyes, draping a simple mantle on athletic shoulders that still carried the hint of puppy fat. These boy wonders would leave the presence of their imperial protector to spend the day fortifying their young spirits and minds with Homer. After which they would perfect their budding bodies with noble exercise. Finally at midday and under the eyes of the emperor they would demonstrate their promise of manhood in contests of strength and skill. Glistening with oil, in the heat of the sun those tarts paraded like imitation Greek heroes. O how Hadrianus loved to embellish, to make those boys reflect his glory… at least for a while. And of course when clouds of hair began covering the sun of the boy's beauty, Hadrian would realize that it was time to impart his powers to another yet more deserving boy. Yesterday's youth who had the audacity to grow older and become a man (oh, the curse of aging) would be exiled to the obscurity out of which he arose.

After all a game is a game. At the risk of sounding catty, Hadrianus loves to play games, after all they are so dramatic and repetitive, almost eternal. Despite Hadrianus' overheated imagination, nobility was not the game they were playing. Far from being the scions of noble Greek lords, they rose out of obscure backgrounds. Chosen not so much for noble virtue as noble physiques; they were plucked with some tenderness, like mushrooms (who would want to damage the merchandise?) from the corners of the empire. Their families were invariable excited at the broadening scope and influence of their sons. After all if you are a wine merchant from Caeserea or Bithynia and your son has the opportunity to serve the Lord of the World, wouldn't you jump at the chance?

The boys would come to Rome to go to page school. Though Hadrianus imagined something different, they simply became highly prized boys treated to the good life. Traveling around Rome in special carriages, their delicate complexions protected from the climate by precious ointments, their bodies provocatively clad in shear tunics; they wore gold and silver, and their feet were shod in purple boots that never touched dusty ground. Some sullen Greek freedman would lord it over this juvenile mob and half heartedly attempt to teach them proper Latin and Greek so that each when called to court would not only look beautiful but sound it.

Antinous was one of those darling page boys, plucked from Bithynia during Hadrianus' incessant travels. I was the one who first noticed Antinous at the palaestra. Yes, I was there with dear Pedanius watching the boys, not so much for my own pleasure, I am a stoic after all, but I was always on the lookout for the next favorite. It was a game Hadrianus and I played. I would find a boy and get someone else (who would soon be exiled from the court in imperial gratitude) to perform the invaluable service of proposing him to Hadrianus.

Yes, It was a warm muggy day in Bithynia (In spite of what they say, the Black sea is a rather tepid, brackish body of water in summer); like so many small trading cities, the people tend to be wiry and uncouth, fit for business and not pleasure…no real beauties in sight. Then I noticed a rather large boy wrestling with another clearly more aggressive and skilled partner. The big boy did not seem motivated to win, and of course he was vanquished. He stood up all dusty and naked hardly seeming to notice that he had just been defeated...motionless, looking out to that dispirited sea; and then he smiled, not a sneaky or embarrassed smile, but a smile illuminated by some unexpected and mysterious joy. For a moment, I actually felt the pleasure of simply being alive...like a sudden cool breeze. How strange! I wondered if it was something that the presence of the boy did, and more importantly if he would have that affect on our dear emperor.

Though the boy's body was a little thick in the chest, and his neck was too short, indeed there was something a bit foreshortened about him, I decide that he looked altogether charming. And since I did not like Pedanius (I hate sniveling sycophants, even if he is the nephew to the emperor), I decided to point out the potentials of this

possible new imperial protégé. "That boy, yes the one over there standing alone, do you not think that there is something rather fetching about him and yet innocent. Why clean him up a little and he would be absolutely charming. You know how our emperor loves innocence."

Pedanius, a unappealing damp creature with red hair (I wish he would stop playing with his nose; at least he's not my cook.) who was always looking for ways to please his uncle; took the bait. Even with Pedanius's lack of intelligence, he could have survived at the court for a while except for his desperate habit of trying too hard. "Do you think that the boy would really please the emperor? I've got an idea; why don't I mention him to my uncle. He ignores me so. Perhaps if I find him a new boy he'll understand how valuable I can be."

I nodded as reassuringly as I knew how. "What a wonderful idea. Yes, the emperor might very well be pleased with the boy." What I did not say was that the emperor certainly did NOT want anyone to be invaluable, let alone a blood relative. Like I said, I was getting bored with Pedanius. Poor, poor Pedanius.

As planned, the next day Pedanius almost dragged his uncle to the palaestra and pointed out the boy whose name happened to be Antinous. Hadrianus who had just discovered an absolutely valiant looking young Gaul (who I had a former member of the court point out to him), had Antinous sent to page school in Rome to smooth over the rough edges. While the rest of the court continued to bask in the presence of the emperor on that trip, alas, Pedanius was sent back to Rome to deliver his charge. Hadrianus told Pedanius to stay there. Before he left, I sympathized with him for the injustice he suffered. Though he seemed fated for obscurity, he was after all the emperor's only blood relation. I did not survive in the court this long by recklessly burning bridges. All and all, I was rather pleased with my days work. For all my feigned obsequiousness, I towered above them all.

Not that Hadrianus was not magnificent in his own way. After all the empire had been at peace for most of his reign; he had an absolute passion for order, or more precisely a passion for the rules of his game. Until that last trip down the Nile, his world ran admirably.

But to get back to Antinous, I always took a kind of pride in him; you might say that he was my idea. There he was languishing in the page school at Rome, among the polyglot and boisterous mob of all those other boys plucked just like him...a fairly beautiful boy, surrounded by boys at least as beautiful. Though as I said, I took a certain pride in Antinous; I was not blind to his defects. His nose was just a little too thick and in a few years would be downright fleshy. He had a good forehead, high and noble, but his eyes though almond shaped and deep were just a bit small; although his long slanting eyebrows distracted you from this defect. The gap between the base of his nose and his upper lip was curiously short causing that upper lip to arch upward. His lower lip protruded out slightly making his mouth seem a trifle open, moist and promising pleasure like a dewy red rose. There was something preposterous almost clumsy about his beauty.

His hair was a crowning glory though. It was not simply that it was jet black with a kind of violet glow, but it curled loose and wild from his head in an altogether unselfconscious way. It hung there wildly as if its owner were completely unaware of its curling beauty.

Unfortunately as I mentioned before his neck was a little short and his chest too broad. These were ominous flaws, betraying an immanent thickening maturity. Though Bithynia has pretenses of being part of the Greek world, alas, our dear Antinous was far from a classical beauty. But there was a kind of freshness about him, as if he were oblivious to himself and absorbed by the world happening around him. He always had a faint look of surprise on his face, so unlike those other dear boys that surrounded him. There was one particularly charming look of his made all the more alluring by this utter lack of self-consciousness...periodically he would suddenly look up from whatever he was doing, like he had just woken up after a particularly restful sleep...so surprised to see the loveliness of the morning. The smile would start deep down inside him and slowly seep to the surface. His eyes would be out of focus with the faraway look of babies when they are defecating. Time seemed to stand still. Indeed if I had time for such foolishness, I would have considered...

I made a point of observing him frequently. There was a special grill on the east wall of the boys' changing room at the school, through which I was allowed to peek, without being observed. He may have simply been dreamier than the usual adolescent, but somehow when he opened into that smiling, dreamy look of his, I thought that I could see depths of something beyond the ordinary. I think the poor boy bonded with me in some strange and almost pathetic way.

Ironically it was our dear ignored empress Sabina who finally singled Antinous out from the rest of those beauties. Despite my interest in the dear boy, Hadrianus on his own would not have picked Antinous; after all as I said, he was not a classic beauty, and Hadrianus was crazy about the Greek classical age.

Marriage had been such a disappointment for Sabina, even though she had been the niece of Trajan (Hadrianus was so strategic). Not that Roman wives expect romance, but they do expect respect. Hadrianus seemed to want to expose her to contempt; he paraded his fresh heroes-in-the-making around to public occasions. She became older and tighter and more bitter as Hadrianus became more public and grandiose about his latest pubescent wonder. At one point there was even talk (you know how I do not like to share gossip) that that absurd poetess Babilla who thought she was Virgil had a dangerously intimate relationship with Sabina. Hadrianus yanked Babilla away from Sabina and made Babilla his clown/poet. Women had a very incidental place in his games; I suppose again he was imitating the Greek mode.

Rumor has it that Sabina first saw Antinous during one of Hadrianus' in between stages…without a boy. The young pages would be invited to the palace of Hadrianus (of course Sabina had to be there). He would casually examine them for signs of promise. Antinous never showed particularly well; he could even look oafish. He was such an innocent that he also presented himself to the powerless empress and addressed her with great reverence. Whether it was boredom, contempt or even sympathy, Sabina began bestowing her neglected favors on Antinous. Not that anything indiscreet happened.

Though Hadrianus was not interested in his empress, but was careful that no one would be interested in her either (just look at what happened to absurd Babilla). He saw that Antinous became a kind of favorite of Sabina..

Antinous had the failing of being absolutely kind. Just as his hair dangled unselfconsciously for all to see, so his basic kindness. I would not even call it a virtue; virtue takes some cultivation. Not that his teachers did not attempt to show him the importance of directing that affection of his… but after all, perhaps Antinous was a simple boy. Because he piqued my interest, I tried to steer him in the direction of artful machination, but all to no avail. The boy seemed unable to maintain even the slightest strategy.

Even Sabina whose naiveté in entering her marriage to Hadrian was almost legendary, had been able to develop that morose demeanor of hers to fend off humiliation. Sabina certainly could have done much better than marrying Hadrianus, after all she had been the favorite niece of the emperor Trajan when Hadrianus was some vague undistinguished relation, although very dashing in an over blown male kind of way, a man's man. Little did Sabina realize what a man's man he was, or should I say boy's man. Like so many after her, Sabina thought that Hadrianus would owe her a debt of gratitude for making him a more serious contender for Trajan's mantle of authority. When Hadrian eventually triumphed, he did his best to ignore his once useful spouse. She had been invaluable to his success… poor dear.

I suppose even back then Hadrianus had already been bitten by the divinity bug. Not that we would have actually noticed, since he reigned as kind of a fickle god over his court. He seemed to want the whole world to think that he had sprung omnipotent from some godly time that predated mortal memory; that he was of a substance so different from the rest of us that we could not understand him. We must only trust in his endless wisdom. Poor dear Sabina, although, the truth be told, I soon became bored by her constant complaints. Whenever she heard the name of her spouse, she would suck in air and hold it blowing out her cheeks. Just as she was beginning to turn blue, she would release the imprisoned air and hiss it out in stale discontent. Perhaps she was an innocent too, but her foolishness taught me wisdom.

I myself was very self effacing about what little, dare I say, help I gave Hadrian in the writing of his laws. When my lord would invite me to speak with him about my latest superbly written legal masterpiece (I was especially proud of my, I mean Hadrianus' Edict Perpetuam), I would be very, very careful. Hadrian would usually have that unique and uncomfortable look on his face that had replaced what could have been a sense of gratitude. I knew that that look was usually a prelude to exile out to some place like Judea. Now, did I mention that Hadrianus really is intelligent, although not exactly astute? Before any words came out of his mouth, I would bow, looking my most helpless. "My Lord, I am so grateful to you for keeping me as your secretary, as clumsy as I am with language. My spelling, I won't even talk about my spelling. How can you be so kind? Especially with the cost of keeping my house on the Palatine Hill, how can you stand to put up with my incompetence?"

That distasteful look of his would pass, replaced by a benign, tolerant smile. "Julianus, it is not the outcome but the effort that is important." He would nod, self satisfied in my direction and once again I was safe if humbled.

He would have exiled Sabina if he could have, but after all the niece of a former emperor has some rights, be they ever so arid. I have often wondered why she continued to want to tag along with him. I suppose she never gave up hope in some kind of divine justice; no wonder she grew more morose by the day. Her close proximity also allowed Hadrianus to guard her untouched virtue. She had a role to play in his game, and he would make sure that she fulfilled that obligation.

And that is how he discovered Antinous. There was talk at court, actually rumors about the familiarity of our sour empress with the boy from Bithynia. Hadrianus spied on them, hoping at long last to find a reason to eliminate his spouse all together. What he found was a rather touching friendship, two innocents seeking consolation (altogether platonic) in a world far too complex and calculating for them. Hadrianus was charmed, not by Sabina but by this new boy. Hadrianus plucked Antinous out of the unruly mob of beauties and gave him the very temporary role of favorite, despite the far from classical face and body prone to thickening. In reward for bringing this new boy to his attention, he sent Sabina to Brandisium for an indeterminate amount of time…a vacation of course (as if anyone would go to that dismal city for pleasure).

I think that Antinous would have become like all the other beauties, momentarily satisfying Hadrian's hunger for young maleness before being dropped back into obscurity; but something unforeseen occurred. Hadrianus fell seriously ill, not that anyone was supposed to know. He told everyone at court that he was going on a hunting trip on which, by the way, he brought the best physicians of the empire and yours truly. The physicians successfully propped up Hadrian's, dare I say, flagging health for which they were exiled to Armenia. I was of course too inconsequential to be noticed, a kind of shadow.

Though Hadrian had just turned fifty (I guarded that secret carefully), he returned from his invigorating adventure still magnificent, but thinner; and was that fear hiding in his eyes? We all said how well he looked. He began new building projects all over the empire...a bridge here, an aqueduct there...the more that fear grew in his eyes, the more building projects sprouted up across the empire. He began what was to be a villa north of Rome, but its scope and grandeur kept expanding until it looked nothing less than a huge and empty mausoleum. He peopled that villa with galleries of silent and ageless statues.

He also started on what was to be his most grand trip of all, to Greece and Asia and finally Egypt. This time he had Antinous. I really expected the emperor's taste for male variety to increase with his own diminishing powers, but something about the innocence and devotion of the dear boy seemed to satisfy the emperor, or perhaps those moist lips of Antinous were simply too succulent for Hadrianus to pass by (I know that almost trapped me).

We all packed up, at least those of us who were privileged to be invited on the trip. He brought Sabina and Pedanius along, to keep an eye on them; they traveled in the rear in less than imposing circumstances. After all, leaving a wife and a nephew back in Italy with all those plotting senators was not a good idea. Hadrianus also included Julia Babilla. I mentioned her all ready. She was Hadrianus' creature now and all the rage in Rome. Her popularity had gone to her head to such an extent, that she simply wanted to be identified with one name, Babilla. I think that's hubris, or at least I hoped so. Once she found favor with Hadrianus she avoided her precious Sabina. Girls will be girls, or should I say boys will be boys; such a strange creature Babilla is.

She was commissioned to write an epic about the heroic journey of our emperor. She had the annoying habit of reading her plodding and bombastic efforts to me. She thought I liked her poetry. With her large, porcine face, her lumpy body barely covered by some odd colored toga (Why did she insist on wearing men's togas?), she always seemed to be sputtering on about her poetry. Either she was a very poor poet or she was playing my game. Then there were virtually hordes of slaves and servants whose purpose was to silently ensure our comfort.

We set out by ship from Brandisium...first port of call, Athens. During the weeks on board Hadrianus kept us busy with minute directions and grandiose plans. He had always been a perfectionist, but of late he was carrying that a bit far. No detail was beneath his concern: how servants were dressed, how sailors wound there ropes, how food was cooked, as if all of us, his entire fleet were an extension of his demanding, dare I say, failing body. We all praised and thanked him for his deep concern, but in the dark of my cabin, at times I wished, not for exile but a temporary reprieve from his attentions. Fortunately the voice of reason pierced through the melancholic obscurity of my cabin, and I remembered what a very important person (though still very humble of course) I had become. After all, life did not exist outside the radiance of Hadrianus's power; I was at the heart of life.

Our arrival in Athens offered me a respite. The scope of Hadrian's control broadened and perhaps diluted (the day before we docked he was actually showing me the proper way to chew). Either Antinous was stupid, or in love, certainly not calculating; he seemed absolutely entranced by the emperor's directions. In Greece they discovered a common passion, hunting. Each morning they would set out together to explore and find what scanty game was in the hills outside of that city.

After all Hadrianus was fifty, that delicate age where even the healthiest of men begins feeling twinges of mortality. He still looked fairly hardy and vigorous (I will not mention again about that last illness), and each day he set out into the countryside with blooming, eager Antinous. The pace Hadrianus set continued to be a bit shall we say, frantic? He so loved to teach Antinous, and as I said before, Antinous was the most curious of boys. He would look up at his lord and master enthralled by every feat Hadrianus would demonstrate. What was even more bizarre was that Antinous looked sincere. Not that the rest of the court did not try to give the impression of sincerity, but I, the master of dissembling, could tell their timing was always just a bit off. Either courtiers responded just a little too rapidly with praise, as if they actually had not freshly taken in Hadrianus' splendor; or they paused just a moment too long before offering complements, as if they needed time to calculate. Antinous responses were always just right.

Poor Hadrianus, if only he could have remained satisfied with more prosaic beliefs. Give me a lukewarm stoic or a fickle epicurean any day. No… in Athens he began to get involved with Greek mystery cults. Hadrianus, who never had any time for women, became absolutely crazy about the goddess Demeter, queen of mysterious rebirth. Even though many of the vulgar crowd in Rome were shopping the empire for odd and exhilarating new beliefs, I hardly expected it of our emperor. After all we more sober Romans had conquered all those vagaries with our laws. Now those vanquished divinities and rituals were popping up everywhere. That our most rational emperor would indulge in those fantasies was beyond belief...not that I told him so.

In spite of what everybody says, those Greeks are really quite extreme and shall we say wildly irrational. Of course everybody talks about Socrates and Plato and Aristotle, but what your average Greek loves is salvation, and dear Divine Demeter reigns supreme in the desperate and vulgar halls of redemption. Our man Hadrianus started looking to a woman, albeit immortal, to save his soul. Blind as I was back then, I thought that Hadrianus was nodding condescendingly to a primitive belief, the way he would acknowledge a clumsy maid servant. I never dreamed that he actually needed saving, or for that matter, that I did.

So after decimating the game in the vicinity of Athens, still with Antinous in tow, our emperor decided to do the Demeter experience, or more formally, the Great Mysteries of Eleusis. Such imaginations those Greeks have! By report, Demeter the Great Goddess of Nature had a lovely little morsel of a Daughter named Persephone. One day while budding Persephone was playing with her nubile maidens, she saw a beautiful flower in the distance. She escaped the flock of beauties to pluck it. Unfortunately Pluto, the god of the underworld, had designs of the basest sort on Persephone; this flower was part of his grand scheme. When greedy little Persephone clutched the flower, Pluto yanked her down into the netherworld. Poor Persephone, even worse, poor Demeter. She was so grieved that she abandoned Olympus and all her abundance creating magic and roamed the earth grieving her daughter. With Mother Nature on the lamb, earth became desolate. This went on for far too long, at least that is what Zeus thought. Frustrated beyond endurance, he negotiated a peace between Demeter and Pluto. Demeter would have her hardly worse for the wear daughter three seasons of the year. Pluto would have his queen for one season, winter. If the Persephone had been a human, the gods would not have cared.

According to the overheated Greeks, Eleusis is where Persephone stepped back from Hades into the hysterical arms of her mother. So those ever credulous Greeks decided that here at Eleusis, was the font of salvation.

Of course we Romans are too sober for such flights of fancy. We are satisfied with more tangible wonders like aqueducts and coliseums, at least while we are young. As I said before, Hadrianus was far from young, and though his rule of the empire was absolute, the rule of his body was faltering.

Enthusiastically if temporarily, Hadrianus played according to Demeter's rules; he and Antinous joined the ranks of all the other supplicants. The schedule of the ritual was carefully prescribed. The first four days of the mystery were a boyish frolic for the pair. From Athens they would race to the sea by the town of Eleusis, and there by a rocky promontory plunge into the warm Mediterranean accompanied by a small pig. Those Greeks have such a quaint sense of humor. Each day the three frolicked in the sea.

On the fifth day, our two pious heroes joined the common crowd of worshippers in Athens; crowned with wreathes and carrying myrtle branches, they set off for Eleusis in a long procession. Imagine our poor dear emperor surrounded by the masses of common men processing and chanting through the hills of Aigaleos.

Oh dear, I forgot to mention that the day before while the two were still romping into the sea, Hadrianus noticed hair was just beginning to sprout out of the otherwise smooth skin of his Antinous. In the commotion of being saved, Hadrianus did not mention it, or begin making plans.

At any rate, by night fall, the now torch bearing crowd passed over the bridge of Cephisos, which by the way Hadrianus had built (perhaps to ensure that Demeter's arms would open to him). The mysteries may have been Demeter's but the architecture was still his. As per usual masked men hurled insults at the throng. Imagine telling your emperor that his mother was a Corinthian whore. Hadrianus could be such a good sport when he wanted to be. The overly excitable pilgrims now entered the grand courtyard of Eleusis. After three more days of being bombarded with dramas about poor Demeter and far, far too much chanting; the wreaths of the crowd were freshened, and all were clothed in long robes, even our vain emperor (no torso enhancing leather for him today). The frenzied crowd marched into the Teletrion accompanied by gongs and chanting, to experience the climax of this rather overdrawn event. Hadrianus was clearly eating it up, all the while explaining the significance of things to his wide eyed companion. Though of course this was all foolishness to me, even I, who was privileged to accompany them, cannot tell you what happened next. Secrecy is strictly enforced. My balls would turn to marble and putrid boils would form on my face if I actually told you what I saw; you know the fury of those Greek gods. Needless to say Hadrianus was moved by this mystery of death and rebirth, at least that's what he said to Antinous (a word to the wise, Eleusis does not make for a particularly charming weekend). Of course I told the emperor how grateful I was for the opportunity to share in this life changing experience. I was very, very grateful.

Though Hadrianus could not say he was healed, that would imply some previous weakness; he could talk about being transformed, perhaps to some even higher level of grandeur. Mere extremely fallible mortal that I am, I was able to declare some humble level of healing and express my gratitude to him for being included in this misadventure. I silently noticed that in his heightened state of grandeur his eyes burned brighter and his penchant for giving exacting and urgent orders gathered more momentum.

By this time we all could see that hair was beginning to cloud the face of our not so classical beauty, Antinous. We were waiting to hear that the boy or shall we say man was being sent back home to the benighted shores of the Black Sea.

Possibly Hadrianus was too busy to exile his friend. Poor dear middle aged Hadrianus began assuming even more pretensions to immortality. He started an overblown temple to Zeus in Athens. The statue of Zeus looked suspiciously like Hadrianus, or perhaps Hadrianus looked suspiciously like Zeus (things were beginning to get muddled). In his eagerness to consume divinity our emperor seemed to have now forgotten Demeter. His interest in women was very limited after all.

Poor ever so human Antinous was not bearing up particularly well, we all knew he was on borrowed time, and we began transferring our attentions to younger and more likely boys. For all Antinous's purported natural wisdom, the dear boy did not catch the drift. He continued to expect us all to listen to him, and when we did not, that lower lip of his that had stuck out in an endearing pout looked spoiled and foolish on a man who should know better. How did that absolutely charming boy become a grotesquely seductive man? He should have been using what was left of his influence to get sent to a province that was not totally barbarous.

Instead Antinous tried all sorts of desperate maneuvers, he shaved, not just those over ripe cheeks of his, but his whole body. Then the poor boy stopped eating in hopes of delaying the inevitable thickening of his torso. Most of all he pouted, pouted, pouted as only an adolescent can do, one minute pathetic and the next hostile. What happened to that dear boy of the palaestra who I worked so hard to cultivate? Is that gratitude? I should have left him pitting olives in Bithynia.

We all knew that Hadrian and Antinous were not sharing a bed anymore. For the time being Hadrianus did not make a selection of another favorite; he was too busy becoming divine to pay attention to Antinous's antics let alone satisfy his own more human urges. Perhaps in Hadrianus' sentimental middle age he could not let go of his changeling.

We escaped from summer in Athens…hot streets rank with the smell of urine and the clamor of its over rated philosophers. We set sail and stopped at Ephesos. That city, so drunk on myth, turned out to greet Hadrianus, alias Zeus. My, but those Greeks are certainly either mad or quite clever. They hardly seemed to notice that this Zeus looked slightly drawn and was wearing just the hint of make up, and yes, he did have a little limp. Choruses of chanting maidens and scantily clad boys proclaimed the unending majesty of our dear leader. In fact the only time now that Hadrianus did not appear restless was when people were extravagantly praising his divinity. Processions, processions, processions, cymbals and flutes and chanted praises to his endless power were becoming tedious (I got so tired of the smell of incense; I started developing a slight cough).

We set sail for Antioch; even my almost unlimited patience was wearing thin; I started dreaming about retiring to some idyllic place near Neopolis to write my memoirs. We then traveled overland to Jerusalem; I actually had to ride a donkey, my legs will never be the same and that's not even mentioning the dust and the fleas. Even Pedanius was running out of praise, and Babilla kept complaining that she was experiencing some sort of internal impediment to the writing of her epic. Only Antinous seemed to rise to the occasion. The more difficult the journey became, the more pleased he appeared to be at the side of Hadrianus.

We rode through the broken walls of Jerusalem. The people of that miserable city greeted us with silence, as if it were our fault that they had rebelled against Roman power. Though Hadrianus was displeased that the sullen citizens of that city were reluctant to praise him as a god, he decided to help rebuild the city anyway. For starters he ordered a grand temple of Zeus-Hadrianus to be built on the ruins of their shabby little temple. The Roman governor had the ingratitude to suggest that this act might lead to further hostilities. To make up for the governor's lack of loyalty, I praised the wisdom and generosity of Hadrianus and suggested that the governor be replaced. I was back in good form again.

After a short trip overland, we set sail for Alexandria. At the royal harbor we were greeted by a crowd of priests huddled under an enormous canopy slung from the pediment of the temple of Isis. After all the Egyptians are quite used to gods walking among them; not a feat of imagination here, just an every day occurrence. Our god Zeus-Hadrianus now became god Osiris. As we departed the ship led by our emperor, we were engulfed in the sound of clanging symbols and some sort of wailing singing that was supposed to please gods (It sounded more like cats in heat). Again we began days of parading through those broad avenues between the lake and the sea. The Egyptians must be blind to good taste...all the buildings were painted in the most garish of colors (even worse then the Greeks). Even Babina who decked herself out in the most obnoxious of hues was appalled.

And of course the clumsy boy-man Antionous followed close behind his lord, covered with little bloody nicks from his attempts at shaving. All that unnecessary bleeding touched a soft spot in my heart. If I did not have more important things to do, I would have suggested to Hadrianus that perhaps I could have use for Antinous as a chamberlain, or in some other overdressed capacity where he could pretend to some consequence. I was very busy though, and after all, Antinous had disappointed the emperor...all that ridiculous hair, you know. If the emperor is disappointed, so am I.

The dear boy seemed to believe that our emperor should actually continue in this now unseemly relationship. Oh my! Now for a man to share his overflowing largesse with a boy is perfectly acceptable, even expected; but for two men... that is a different story. One of them would have to be in the female role, and Demeter aside, let us face it, the role is clearly secondary and for a man, ridiculous. We all know about those effeminate men who sell their asses to sailors. That our emperor could be involved in such commerce was beyond the pale of propriety, and for our dear emperor it was beyond the pale of his heroic dignity.

The halls of Alexandria rang with the praises of the God Hadrianus; the alleys though were filled with clever ditties about the silly old emperor and the man to whom he was enthralled. We in the court did not mention those rumors to Hadrian. The whole idea of Hadrianus spreading his legs to make way for the some thickening of another man was more than preposterous; it was very dangerous. Though the priests of Alexandria continued in their effusive praise, even our intelligent but not very acute emperor must have heard unexplained laughter from the crowd.

Now Alexandria, except for all those garish temples and yawling priests, is the Greekest of cities these days, and if Antinous were still a hairless boy, his company would have added to the luster of Hadrianus's virility. Unfortunately even with daily shaving, their was a telltale black shadow over Antinous' face and limbs, not to mention the scabs. Even worse he was broadening at an alarming rate, actually becoming burly. It seemed that as Antinous reluctantly waxed virile, Hadrianus waned until he seemed a mere slice of his former self.

That is when Hadrianus heard about a lion west of Alexandria that was ravaging the countryside. Perhaps our diminishing emperor saw it as an opportunity to enhance his flagging heroic stature. The more he talked about the impending hunt, the lion became bigger and more ferocious until truly it was a fitting adversary for a god. Our party set out into the desert proudly led by our heroic leader. We watched our emperor become more vital; even Antinous stopped pouting and looked excited. For a while Hadrianus and Antinous again became two adventuring boys, Hadrian explaining to him about tracking lions, Antinous listening enthralled. Then they would ride off together almost like friends. Even though this companionship no longer made sense to any of us, I decided that I better not ignore Antinous too quickly, who knows? After all we are dealing with a god, albeit a failing one.

Two days out we came upon the lion's latest kill, a young boy mauled and gutted by the beast. Our emperor knelt known next to the remains of the still warm corpse. His nostrils flared; all his senses seemed to open up. He listened for something that none of us could hear. Suddenly he glanced at Antinous and ran towards his horse. I hardly noticed his limp. Antinous raced after him smiling and eager to follow a fresh trail. The rest of us, Pedanius, Babilla, myself, and our usual entourage of nobodies followed far enough back to be out of immediate danger, close enough to view the heroic encounter from a fitting distance. After all Babilla had an epic to write.

We were just making our way (I was on a scratchy, smelly mule again) over a dry and stony rise, and our two intrepid adventurers seemed to have cornered something in a dusty thicket at the bottom of a ravine. We kept our vantage point, stationed at a perfect distance to take in the whole scope of our emperor's bravery. They both jumped off their horses and grabbed their spears and stood five feet apart like brave comrades...they stealthily approached the thicket. They were crouched down bracing themselves as if at any moment the force of the lion could sweep over them...there I saw it, a rather old beast, perhaps like Hadrianus. At first it cowered and began snarling as it backed against what looked like a large rock. It was making a last stand, shaking its mangy head. Even from this distance its eyes looked frightened; and then it let out one last defiant roar...what marvelous entertainment! Choosing the weaker of its two assailants, it charged toward our emperor. Hadrianus set his feet more solidly on the stony ground and cocked his spear back. From a distance I could see the spear sailing out of his hand and glancing off the lion's shoulder. For the briefest of moments Hadrianus looked at the lion with what must have been disbelief, then he turned and began frantically scrambling, limping away...he stumbled. With absolute calmness, Antinous cocked his spear back and threw it straight and true into the neck of the lion; blood spurted out in a rain of red. The emperor lay flat on his face still waiting for the jaws of the lion to crush him.

Pedanius poked Babilla with his elbow and smiled in delight. I am more cautious and looked appropriately shocked; that was the best strategy when facing a fallen god. I had been with our emperor too long not to be horrified at the situation that I now faced. I had witnessed the forbidden.

We his servants approached the scene in a herd; I alone seemed to recognize the danger and walked slightly behind my naive companions. Our emperor pulled himself up, his right knee had been gashed by his fall, and walked over to the spasming lion. Just as we were closing in, Hadrianus slit the beast's throat with his sword and positioned himself over the lion.

I had survived the courts of Domitian, Nerva, and Trajan. I knew now that I faced a dilemma far more dangerous than a rampaging lion. I witnessed the emperor's failure. Did I tell you that I pride myself on my sophistry? Out of confidence in my skill and from behind the bulk of Babilla I spoke barely audibly.

"My lord Emperor, you are more than a hero and indeed worthy of Olympus. I saw your generosity to your poor servant Antinous. You gave a glancing blow to that lion, in order that your humble servant could have an opportunity, to kill the beast. Only a god could be that generous. Unfortunately your poor servant's aim wasn't true, and you needed to vanquish the beast yourself. People will be talking about this exploit as long as the pyramids stand."

Fortunately Hadrian appeared to be in such a daze that he hardly noticed that I was the author of this face saving story.

Antinous had been smiling with pride as we approached, but as I uttered my praise he looked with confusion at

Hadrianus. The poor boy wanted praise and gratitude. Clearly he did not realize how Hadrianus treated people who helped him. As much as I was ready for Antinous's replacement, I did wish that he could have played along...I knew that it would have been easier on him in the long run.

Antinous looked straight at our emperor, and simply said, "Hadrianus?"

Our dear Babilla covered up the moment. She stepped closer to the emperor so that she could get his attention and make proper impact. I became inconspicuously absorbed in straightening my sandal, pretending that I was not there. Dressed in strange shade of red, the color of raw pork kidney, she began reciting, impromptu, the epic of Hadrian's triumph over the lion and how he saved the life of Antinous. Such a dear she was, but shall we say a bit overly ambitious. Now that Hadrianus had gathered his wits, he could see that Babilla was the one who was responsible for saving his face. I was much too busy to have noticed anything. She began singing.

> "I sing of war and a hero, driven by
> His destiny to travel to the shores
> Of Africa, and the sufferings
> Of this, the first adventurer, by sea
> And land, impelled by heaven's will
> Blah, blah...blah, blah...blah."

I did not want to deflect the emperor's gratitude from Babilla by suggesting that this sounded suspiciously like Virgil.

Pedanius, eager to get his licks in, spoke, "My lord, in the fierce struggle with the BEAST, your noble knee was torn. The whole empire is in awe at the divine blood you shed for us all. We are grateful that you would sacrifice your divinity for our feeble humanity!" Pedanius was literally fluttering in excitement.

As usual Hadrianus did not need to say anything. Aside from his Olympian nods, he said little those days unless he deigned to impart some bit of wisdom. He always did have a rather pompous style which had been further aggravated by his ascent to divinity. He nodded at Babilla and Pedanius in uncomfortable and dangerous gratitude. Fortunately as I said before, I was camouflaged by Babilla's raw pork colored attire.

That annoying lower lip of Antinous began sticking out in the most petulant of manners. The boy-man seemed disturbed at our handling of reality...he kept looking at Hadrianus in that unappealing way of his. The poor boy did not realize that emperors create their own truths. Or I could wade into a pool of sophistry and say we all create our truths, but some peoples' are so much more important; but I do not want to start becoming philosophical…look what happened to Socrates. I have always chosen to stay with the herd...like a sheep in a flock, a flock for which our emperor has particular, condescending fondness...our dear shepherd.

To make a tedious story short, Hadrianus triumphantly returned to Alexandria with that sullen boy following him looking for someone to say he was right; it's a wonder Hadrianus put up with him, although our emperor can be so kind to miscreants. Besides page school was a Mediterranean away, and frankly those boys of Alexandria were too effeminate for male worshipping Hadrianus. Though he seemed to be melting away in the Egyptian sun, he was able to maintain divine benevolence towards Antinous, of course with our support. The nasty gossips of Alexandria whispered that the emperor's sexual prowess had evaporated just like that over-drawn musculature of his.

As if the lion outing were not unfortunate enough (by the way did I mention that Hadrianus was so grateful to Babilla about that epic that he exiled her to Germany... poor ambitious dear), he decided that he must take a trip up the Nile. It seemed the annual flood had been dreadfully disappointing last year, and grain stores were getting low. As the god Osiris, our emperor believed that he could assure the flood this year (He did seem to actually believe that). So the whole entourage was packed up into barges; at least I did not have to ride a mule. Sabina who had been laying low and not doing anything to entice Hadrian's dangerous gratitude was permitted to remain in Alexandria. She seemed relieved. How could she relinquish her place in the sun with such serenity? She had been wistfully talking of late about spending her final years at the villa in Compania that her father had given her long ago. She certainly was getting morose (She is younger than I am).

Although if I am absolutely honest (which is always a mistake), I would have to admit that there was something misguided about this whole venture, but at least I was invited along. So there! Indeed the whole of Egypt was sullen that fall. Even with the new Osiris sailing up the Nile, the flood so far that year had been a meager, desultory event. As our splendid barges sailed past the banks of the Nile, the peasants looked at us expectantly as if we could do something about the drought. What would happen if there was a second year of meager flood, the Nile barely filling its banks? Already Egypt was having difficulty gathering enough grain to send to Rome. Fortunately the peasants are used to eating very little, although I suppose that they have limits too. This was certainly not a good year to be Osiris. One particularly naive and unappealing looking man (so skinny) standing on the bank of the Nile as we passed, actually pointed to his dry fields and his squalid family huddled near him and then began screaming at us as we passed by, dining. These Egyptians certainly have something to learn about politeness and reverence.

The whole country thought our dear emperor was neglecting his duty as Osiris. The life giving floods did not seem to be coming, another divine failure...shades of the lion hunt. Was it not enough that we were among them eating their fare which I must say was far below our usual standards? This time Antinous could not be blamed and our bombastic epic creating Babilla had already departed. All I could do was to keep telling Hadrianus what a privilege it was for me, a poor scribe that I am, to accompany his magnificence. I actually began rather wishing that I had come down with some brief, innocuous but frightening disease so that I could return to Alexandria. Perhaps I could share Sabina's less demanding company there for a short while.

What a horrendous journey! I had to walk the sword edge between being helpful and not too helpful. It seems gods are even touchier than emperors. To tell the truth, which is always a mistake (I hope I am not repeating myself), after several months of being at the beck and call of Hadrianus, I was beginning to feel fatigued. After all our emperor kept raising the stakes, first he was the ruler of the world, then he was the immortal favorite of Demeter, then Zeus king of gods, and finally Osiris god of the Nile and the afterlife. Instead of being pleased by all this divinity that he was accumulating, he was becoming more peevish by the mile.

That fall we kept working our way ever farther up the Nile, the sky a bitter, dusty gray, a dank night time chill penetrating our boats, and all the while hungry peasants watched us, waiting, waiting for the flood. It was October

the anniversary of the death and resurrection of Osiris...
more importantly the last chance for the much needed flood.

People have such silly beliefs. Osiris according to the
story was murdered in October, after which dolorous event,
his dear mother/lover collected all the grizzly pieces of his
body to reassemble as a god. Osiris became not only god of
the after life but of the annually rising flood.

Hadrianus in his present state of mind took this story
very seriously. Just as he could not believe that he had not
thrown his spear truly, each morning he would get up and
in disbelief stare at the river that refused to rise. I knew that
by all means I should not witness his disappointment. I let
it be general knowledge that I had a mild case of river fever
and had to stay confined in my quarters each morning.

We were all sick and tired of Antinous, I hated to see
a grown man make a fool of himself. He would stand out
on the deck all day, his skin turning red and horny like
cooked shrimp. When Hadrianus would come on deck for
a moment, Antinous would look up with that eager boy
like expression of his. Occasionally Hadrianus would allow
Antinous to serve him. We all complemented the emperor
on his generosity.

Halfway to Thebes now, everyone but Hadrianus had
despaired of the flood that year...eyes from shore accused
us. We began eating inside the cabins of our boats. Oh to be
at the mercy of silly superstition. No more chanting flower
strewing crowds as we docked; we were treated like a party
of imposters. Between the peasants on shore and Antinous
in the boat, this trip had become a nightmare. All those
fields that would not know a harvest...pity, but not our fault.
The peasants seemed to begrudge the miserable food with
which they supplied us each time our flotilla docked. Did
not they understand that we were used to much better fare?

I stared listlessly into the river and saw my reflection. The trip must have surely taken its toll. I looked so much older. Instead of looking composed, which I am sure I was, the reflection look apprehensive, almost hysterical. Its skin had a greenish cast, like it has some sort of liver or stomach problem.

Julian stared into the bathroom mirror. His stomach suddenly made an ominous rumbling sound. He clenched his teeth as his face turned a greenish hue, sweat beading on his brow. He turned from the mirror pushing himself away from the sink; he had a marriage to attend.

CHAPTER 31

Across town, Tony stands in front of the mirror in his bedroom, naked and vulnerable. With doomsday humor he looks at the youthful breath-taking image. He slowly walks over to the bureau and opens a drawer. He gently lifts the white cloth lying there and delicately unfolds it. He stares at it softly, examining it as if he were remembering something long ago and filled with sadness.

Once again Mother pushes her cart of junk up to Julian's house. She quietly stands in the front yard. Cleo and Jerome scramble after. Jerome stops suddenly and Cleo bumps into to him. He looks deeply offended. "Woman, the source of all human misery!"

Cleo hisses back, "You heretic-burning monster!"

Mother watches. "Children, be attentive. Stop chattering, listen for the rhythm. Then let go, be there. It'll be your turn soon enough."

Though they are still eyeing each other angrily, they stop.

Tony, now, stands in the doorway dressed in a simple white tunic. He looks at mother. "It's time?"

She nods gently. "It's your time."

In a city bus a very plain looking eight year old girl sits stiffly in her drab dress holding a black Bible on her lap. She sits next to an older woman dressed just as drably who is devoutly reading from her Bible.

Through the windows, the dusky streets stream by. City lights are coming on. Only the girls darting eyes betray her curiosity. The bus is empty except for two teenagers giggling in a seat at in the rear and the large male bus driver poured into his seat, sullenly driving.

The bus stops; the girl's eyes dart to the front of the bus. Mother steps onto the bus and serenely slides a dollar bill in to the fare machine. She watches it disappear with fascination.

The bus driver shoots an irritated glance at her. She smiles back and catches the little girl's glance, waves, walking toward her.

The little girl turns away abruptly.

Jerome, dressed like a bishop shoots onto the bus after Mother. Irritated he slips a dollar into the machine. He is muttering, "Sacrilegious, that I have to pay for this…there was a time…." He catches sight of the two teenagers in the back of the bus, laughing and flirting with each other; he storms to the back of the bus.

Cleo, dressed as an Egyptian queen, seductively slides her dollar into the machine, shaking her head at Jerome. "He's no fun, no fun at all."

The bus driver watches her hungrily.

She sits right behind him.

Finally Tony, in his white tunic, steps onto the bus, sliding his dollar into the machine; he looks frightened.

Mother silently sits across the aisle from the girl.

Mother smiles as the girl's eyes dart in her direction. "You always did dress in drab colors, Eleanor."

The girl looks confused and startled, "How do you know my name?"

From the back of the bus, Jerome's voice rings out. "Better that your eyes be poked out than you look at a woman with filthy desire."

Mother shakes her head as she looks straight at the girl. "Children….so busy with their plans. They all want to be pharaohs, bishops or Joan of Arc. Pity they don't like the bit parts; they're more lively. They learn more."

The girl's are glued on Mother now.

Mother nods knowingly. "People need to scale back a little to learn anything. Do you catch my drift Eleanor?"

"But how do you know my name?" Anger and curiosity play across her face; she can't take her eyes off this strange lady.

"You and Franklin certainly had your work cut out for you…The Great Depression…Hitler…Hirohito…the Daughters of the American Revolution."

For a moment, the girl looks like a careworn older woman. She starts talking. "I never felt like I could measure up. I was so homely. What man would want me? I tried so hard to be a good mother, but there was so much I wanted to do for people."

The girl's mother tears her eyes away from her Bible for a minute. "Eleanor, leave that woman alone. I'm sure she has better things to do than listen to your foolishness."

Mother winks at Eleanor. A large billboard with two beautiful people posing next to each other under the caption, "BE A LEGEND IN YOUR OWN TIME." Mother points it out to Eleanor and nods knowingly.

The bus now passes between large institutional buildings that crowd out the sky. There is a bridge ahead.

Mother pulls the chord and nods to Eleanor. "We get out here." She stands up glancing at her children.

Eleanor starts transforming into a young girls again; the bus stops. Mother bends down toward Eleanor and whispers reassuringly, "No one gets left behind…ever."

A Eleanor smiles in relief.

CHAPTER 32

I didn't completely feel myself, but my discipline and sense of purpose impelled me out of that building and under the bridge and toward the river, each step motivated by some inner urge, not just duty, but something as deep as my rebellious stomach. That feels better…the cool air brushed across my chest; the toga fluttering as fast as my heart.

It is evening. What an absurd time for a wedding. It must be some kind of sophomoric joke…to think that Sabina would go along with it. Besides I think of the river as a kind of infection of wildness in our somewhat orderly cities. I walked down from the River Road, down some precarious steps under some overhanging trees, and there up ahead was a large boat anchored at the shore. My absurd colleagues dressed in roman drag were milling about aimlessly. I knew that they have need of my firm but sensitive sense of order. If this is going to be a fiasco, at least we could maintain some sense of decorum.

"Hey Julian…great knees!" It was Babs, dressed in a fushia colored toga, instead of a woman's chiton.

For a moment I almost looked down at my knees, but then decided not to give her the satisfaction (after all this whole mess was her fault...if she hadn't had the hubris to invite Sabina to listen to her poetry that night at the Coffee Grounds, why, I would be sitting peacefully at home perusing documents and even more importantly, my junior colleague would be no more deranged than usual...certainly not getting married to this stupid stud). I shook my head at her, smiling, my eyes accusing her of infamy. Finally I spoke. "Cross dressing my dear? I didn't know they made tents in that color."

That absurd Babs suddenly became serious, staring at me with misguided concern. "Are you all right Julian? You look very pale." She watched me with something like pity... as if I need her help.

"I am absolutely fine...do not be so silly!"

She cocked her head slightly still looking at me, not unkindly I suppose, but I had this odd feeling that she was looking through me. What absurdity!

Benighted by her folly, was she. What more could I do? Some people are simply lost. I smiled at her kindly, "My dear, underneath your tasteless flamboyance, do I see the green eyes of envy?"

Bab's large face studied me for a minute certainly not as ashamed as it should be. "Have a good day Julian." She almost sounded like she meant that. After all she didn't have the intelligence to be sarcastic. Then she walked away to join a crowd of more quietly dressed Romans.

I stood alone valiantly facing the elements...no one seemed to notice me; it was almost like people were avoiding me. I walked up to the large boat...dare I say a ship? As it gently rocked, back and forth, back and forth, it appeared to shimmer, fading in and out of the evening. I must have still been under the influence of that raw pig flesh. As if to answer me, my stomach convulsed again.

There…Sabina approached surrounded by a bevy of Roman maidens, at least they were supposed to be maidens. Surely she should have led her little flock towards me to pay her respects, after all I am her mentor. Everyone began clapping, as those faux virgins passed by not even pausing to acknowledge my presence. Babs rushed up and hugged Sabina. Peder pale and skinny, looking for the life of me like someone freshly dug out of the ground, sneered at Sabina. Even though I realized that she was not going to notice me, I did not think she deserved contempt.

Gathering my wounded but still valiant pride, I walked over to her and with just a hint of reproach said, "Hello my dear you look positively grand, like a Roman empress… ravishing."

For a moment she put her short fingered hand over her mouth to stifle what looked like a startled gasp. Perhaps she was coming to her senses. Then she returned to her more blissful about-to-be married self. She smiled and waving her hand like some beauty queen on a passing float. Babs hovered in the background watching. It made me uncomfortable to have her watching, as if she had stumbled onto something that I had not yet seen…how ridiculous!

I simply noded. Suddenly I realized that my right nipple was exposed to that August evening air. The few hairs surrounding it, gray and curly; I was just about to try to reposition my toga, when I glance up to see a troop of what looks like young centurions approaching. Towering above them in the very center stood the golden Hadrian (now why did I call him that?), expressionless and powerful, leading his troops to this encounter. He was dressed in purple. All heads bow as he approached; it must have been a trick of the setting sun but the boat seemed to become more vivid and brilliant. Now, he was in our midst.

His deep voice bellowed out, "Splendid. We are almost set." That golden amulet (yes that WAS the amulet that Tony gave me), seemed to radiate light and power as it rested against his muscular chest, as if it had a life of its own. He glanced over at Sabina and seemed to notice that Babs was hovering nearby. He fixed his eyes on her…she started to back away from Sabina, paused for a moment and with determination returned. Something else caught Hadrian's attention.

Hadrian's eyes were now focused on a group of people in the distance. Though he did not seem like a man to wait, he stood gazing at their approach as still as a statue.

I, like all the rest, followed the direction of his gaze. I had the sensation of the ground trembling beneath me as I recognized Mother in the lead, dressed in her eccentric mixture of Earth Mother, Virgin Mary, and bag lady. For all her excess flesh she moved lightly, hardly stirring the grass on which her bare feet strode. Behind her marched Jerome. He wore a gown and some sort of bishop's hat, still carrying the briefcase in his hand that promised salvation at the price of four easy installments of $19.95. With the voluptuousness of a cat, Cleo followed. Snowy white linen pleats fell delicately from her shoulders. Below her waist a dark triangle of hair was visible through the very fine and shear linen. On her head she wore a diadem, a golden cobra arching out above her forehead. She carried a scepter in her hand and smelled so strongly of attar of roses that even from a distance it saturated the evening.

And last Tony hesitantly followed, his hair cascading in black curls. Flowers were wound in that newly clean and luxurious mass. He wore a simple tunic as he moved with the unconscious grace of a young man. As they approached more closely, I could see his face, no longer frightened, entranced in some sort of inner focus, almost ecstasy.

Hadrian watched the four approach. He nodded toward the boat. Only a slight nod it was, but that was all that we needed. As he and his troop of centurions marched up the gang plank, we followed like a docile flock of sheep. I wanted to walk over to Tony, to tell him not to get any closer; maybe I'd even bring him home where he belonged. I took a step in his direction. As if Hadrian could read my mind, his arms stretched to pull some imaginary bow as he pointed an arrow at me...I stopped absolutely paralyzed. Then he turned his threatening hands to Tony and released the arrow. Everyone including myself turned our attention to the target. For the life of me, Tony stood like some St. Sebastian, body pierced by Hadrian's gesture, eyes in sacrificial ecstasy looking up perhaps as far as heaven. Besides, I had my job to do, tidying up that crowd; they were very sloppily following Hadrian's directions.

Mother and her family now waited on the bank, absolutely still, their forms darkening in the twilight.

While the river coursed beneath our feet, we all stood in silence waiting for Hadrian's directions. I heard a laugh from that group of shadows on the shore. I could tell it was Cleo. Her sarcastic voice rang out. "This isn't the Nile, but I guess it'll have to do." For a moment whatever spell Hadrian was casting dissipated...instead of an emperor, I found myself staring at a burly young man who seemed at a loss for words, tongue too thick to readily trip over consonants.

Then that sycophant Pedanius (I must have really been sick to call Peder that exalted name) approached Hadrian in abject submission. "Domine non sum dignus...Domine non sum dingus... Domina non sum dignus." Once again Hadrian's spell began transforming the night, freezing it to stillness. Fog seemed to be gathering around the ship now.

I could just barely see Tony's shadowy form separate from his family. In his white tunic he seemed like a moth drawn irresistible towards the boat now glowing in the dismal fog.

As he approached the glowing ship pulsed. For an instant the pulsing seemed to be in rhythm with my pulsing stomach. I sealed my lips ever so tightly.

Tony walked up the plank solemnly, entering the still world. As the shore, indeed that world with which I was familiar, disappeared in the fog, I realize that the boat could be anywhere or nowhere. Hadrian nodded and more torches were lit. He fixed his eyes on Tony with a kind of desperate hunger. Those eyes and the bird on his chest flamed in the darkness.

As Tony stepped onto the ship I heard Agnes scold him, "At least try to look happy. You know how he hates it when you mope."

Tony now stood on the deck, motionless; his eyes trying to evade the flames of Hadrian's eyes. Then slowly and inevitable Tony began being drawn to those flaming green eyes. When both their gazes met, the boat exploded with light.

Hadrian, his voice aching in need, spoke first. "Salve Pulcher Antinous. Welcome to my world. Everything is perfect." He paused and smiled tenderly. 'This is where you belong. This where you have always belonged."

Tony tore his gaze away from Hadrian.

"Is this how the last god of the ancient world greets his creator?"

Tony still looking away, his voice ringing in sadness responded, "Domine, I failed to become a god as you failed to become a man."

For an instant Hadrian looked confused, almost

vulnerable. Stars and city lights and traffic sounds began breaking through the fog. No one seemed to notice except myself and that fool Babilla. Some kind of vague understanding filtered across her silly face. Then I watch her very determinedly step next to Sabina.

Sabina was looking wild…angry, startled, bewildered, as if struggling to understand something that she could not grasp.

Babilla, actually looking heroic, rested her hand on Sabina's trembling shoulder.

The voice of Pedanius called out, "Lord of the world, we salute you!"

The whole crowd started booming, "Lord of the world we salute you!"

The city sounds and lights began diminishing, the outside world once again evaporating.

Hadrian's eyes bore into Antinous. I ruled the world; I rule the world." He looks with satisfaction at the subservient crowd around him. He commanded Antinous, "Do not disappoint our guests."

Antinous bows his head and said, "You never did listen. "

Hadrianus smiled dismissively. "But, that is all there is…you and I, forever. The rest are phantoms called up to serve us. I would have easily left them behind…foolish petty jealous creatures, not like us."

Antinous steadied his gaze. "I am one of those foolish, petty persons." He paused standing silently, the moment stretching out. The boat and all its passengers began to shimmer like an oil slick.

Pedanius chanted, "Domine non sum dignus." The crowd joined in, the boat stopped shimmering and came into focus again.

. Hadrian approached Antinuous and took his hand with

exquisite tenderness, leading him to the edge of the boat. He pointed to the reflection of the boat in the water. It floated there, the image of an ancient Egyptian ship, pulsing in light. As I looked deeper into that fantastic image I could make out the two images of the mighty Hadrianus and the beautiful Antinous…I recognized them, different, yet the same. I could not tear my eyes away. Hadrianus gazed with such terrible passion at Antinous. "You are so beautiful, so perfect!"

As I looked down I saw another image, an image of a calculating old man dressed as an ancient Roman (could this be, could this be me?). Though the eyes of this image seemed alert, glancing all around, they were strangely cold and empty. He was a mere husk. Everything around me blurred; the air rushing through my entrails. My stomach lurched as time raced through me. The saliva in my mouth turned sour. My stomach twisted, a loud guttural sound echoed through body. Oddly enough the radiant image of the boat flickered ever so lightly with my gastric distress.

Tony tore his eyes away from the reflection of the boat, turning in my direction, "Perfection?" Somehow I knew Tony was looking for something from me. I felt too ashamed to turn towards him, and I didn't even remember why. Imagine, I, Julianus, am ashamed. Somewhere in the distance I heard what sounds like Babilla's voice whisper, "It's now or never." But all my intelligence was useless, I did not understand what I was supposed to do next, let alone why this was all happening.

As my stomach roiled, all I could see was the image of that desiccated calculating man, myself. He and I are one, my god he and I are one! And I am inhabiting that creature, thinking with his thoughts, telling his story, living in his world. Now he, now I spoke.

"Did I mention that our dear Pedanius had somehow managed to return bringing another boy with a large adams apple sticking out of his scrawny neck. Pedanius should have just bided his time, but instead taunted Antinous at every opportunity, they all did. Though Hadrianus seemed relatively tolerant of Antinous, Hadrianus became more irritable by the mile with Pedanius. Did our divine emperor have some lingering attraction to Antinous or was he simply appalled at the possibility of bedding this new boy?

Could Hadrianus even have some feeble affection for Antinous, some sort of plain mortar of feeling, a mortar so ordinary and human that he could never admit it? Great architect that he was, he must have known that even the highest and most glorious of his vaulting ceilings were held in place by humble cement. I must have been on that journey too long to think such foolish and sacrilegious thoughts. After all, my job was to humbly praise the towering magnificence of Hadrianus, an eternal magnificence springing forever from itself.

To get back to the trip, we picked up another passenger just south of Heliopolis, a gaunt looking Egyptian magician... he came aboard with the supplies from some miserable village. Perhaps those stingy villagers were hoping that this fool would distract us from the pittance they offered. Hadrianus did need distraction though. This obvious peasant called himself by the absurd name of Pancrates of Alexandria. He was dressed in dirty linen and wore a tall black hat that must have been a peasant's conception of the latest style of Persian Magi. Though we only had five courses that night and the wine tasted like donkey sweat (not that I ever actually tasted animals' excretion, you know how careful I am to avoid contamination), that pseudo magician entertained our emperor for hours, calling up spirits, telling fortunes (mostly about Hadrianus' grand and immortal future), and performing miracles on willing peasants. He even declared that he could raise the dead. Some time before we cast off the next morning, our pseudo magician slipped away probably to go back to his fields. He had accomplished his task of distracting the emperor.

That very night, when we stopped at a dirty settlement called Hir-wer (a settlement so small and poor that they hardly had a sheep to give us), Hadrianus decided to demonstrate that he, not Pancrates was the supreme magician. The local people worshiped some primitive god called Bes, their own native god who they had been worshiping even before Osiris. Bes was supposed to ward off danger and promote abundance. After thousands of years of poverty and hunger on this unfortunate bend of the Nile they still held on to their worship. I had to admire those villagers for their determination, but certainly not their intelligence.

It was a gray and lifeless night after another dusty, disappointing day, and mists were rising from the river and the dank marsh from which Hir-wer rose. The emperor had stayed up later than usual (He had started fatiguing so early of late). He had chosen this night to demonstrate a magic trick that Pancrates could only talk about...he was going to raise someone from the dead. Earlier that evening a peasant had paddled up to the flotilla with a mysterious reed covered bundle in the belly of his boat. Hadrianus who seemed excited about this new plaything had servants open the bundle on deck to reveal a corpse from that unfortunate village. Unlike the meager food the village offered us, the corpse was relatively fresh. It had the faint aroma of raw meat and at one time had been a girl child (you know how little they care for excess girls, here or anywhere for that matters). Despite her unfortunate gender, Hadrianus was to bring her back to life.

Now she rested on the misty trembling deck as if asleep. For a moment I envied her. She did not have to do anything but lay there, no longer wrestling with the dreams of the gods.

But I was on alert. I knew Pancrates' miracles were tricks in which only a mystery hungry person like Hadrianus would believe. I noticed the silliness of that imperial hunger, but kept that information as a useful secret. The real problem was the fact that I would be a witness to his unsuccessful attempt to raise the dead, in other words be a witness to his failure. I needed to have some sort of plan. This would be even more dangerous than the lion hunt. What to do? After this failure my very presence would remind Hadrianus of his, shall we say, limitations; yet I could not noticeably save the day and be known as the person who helped him save face...goodbye Rome, hello some dismal province. My life would be ended. Oh the tragedy of it all.

The whole court sat around the flickering oil lamp and that pale bluish corpse. Was that the sickening sweet smell of rot beginning to rise like the mist, or was that the smell of my fear? Slaves parted the crimson curtains of Hadrianus cabin, and out popped our emperor dressed very much like Pancrates, not that I would have mentioned that to Hadrianus. He prides himself on being utterly original. He had the lumbering Antinous behind him, perhaps on the last adventure on which he would accompany his master.

The poor boy looked, not exactly sullen, just withdrawn, almost contemplative, like he was pondering something. Now, scheming is an essential skill, but thinking too deeply… that is dangerous. Perhaps after all, the dear boy was not very bright, and that introspective look he had was purely instinctual, like a flower bending toward the light. He would not even make a good major domo...pity.

Hadrianus, whispering absurd phrases that sounded suspiciously like the nonsense Pancrates mumbled, walked over to the corpse. His eyes were fixed on the heavens in discourse with some divine force up there, as if there still existed some potent divinity that he had not cannibalized. He stood over the head of the child, and Antinous knelt at her feet. The dear boy's eyes were fixed on his hero. Then Hadrianus gesturing as if he were brushing away gnats (very solemnly though), actually touched that ripening corpse. He let out a fierce yawl to the sky. Was he praying to some sky born deity or simply warning that god, that he was about to be consumed. What an appetite our emperor had.

The stubborn girl child refused to stir. For several minutes we were all absolutely quiet on the boat. Finally people started restlessly shuffling their feet. Someone had the audacity to clear his throat. The emperor stood frozen, only his eyes betrayed confusion. Antinous seemed oblivious to the danger we all faced; his countenance simply kept opening, opening until it was so expanded and fragile collapsing of its own accord. Though his ability to be naive was almost limitless, even he had reached the boundary of the incredible.

Something needed to be done soon or we all faced a life far from the benevolence of our emperor-god. Was this to be my final payment for all my years of service?

Now I would not call it divine inspiration, I have learned too much to make that claim, let me simply say I discovered an opportunity, or rather it discovered me. I looked up into the sky above the child's head and saw stars, yes stars breaking through the gloom. My hand almost on its own began reaching upward, and my finger pointed to some point, any point in the firmament. Hadrianus would be too preoccupied to notice whose hand that was; I whispered to Pedanius next to me. "There's a new star in the sky, our emperor has brought the girl back to life as a star."

Pedanius ever eager and also not very bright did the rest. He announced in an excited voice this newly wrought miracle. "Our divine lord has brought this humble girl back to life. See that bright star to the west...there, right there! Our emperor has cast the soul of the girl into the sky, so that not only we, but all history will know the divinity of the God Hadrianus. All praise Hadrianus!"

Of course everyone followed suite making sure that they were crouched behind Pedanius. In one relieved voice we all chanted, "Divinity is among us, divinity is among us!"

Carefully massed together and in awe, we kept mouthing all sorts of praise for this god among us. Just as important we kept repeating Pedanius's name. It appeared no one liked him, or maybe liking has nothing to do with it. We were simply casting one of our own out as a sacrifice to our emperor's divinity. Pedanius was drunk with his success and stepped toward Hadrian, "Divine uncle are you not pleased with me?"

Hadrianus took one long look at his nephew, and simply walked back into his chamber. We all kept our distance from Pedanius. How proud he was; how relieved the rest of us were, once again saved. Before the night was over Pedanius was informed that he was to be sent back to Italy, and then to some rocky island just south of Sardinia. Since he was the royal heir, it would have been much too dangerous to send him to a restless province.

People fled to their chambers, recklessly I stayed up on the deck alone, sitting quietly in the darkness counting my lucky stars. In my relief I simply sat there hardly caring to make another plan. And yes, even I had a brief moment, as the barge gently swayed and the stars rocked in the sky, a moment in which I seemed to forget all my careful plans. For a few foolish minutes I did not care about my position at court.

My solitary moment was disturbed by two voices. I suddenly felt naked and alone. Why had I allowed myself to be singled out like this? It is not that I mind overhearing people. In fact I have made a fine art of that. It is simply that I hate being discovered eves dropping. I crouched down and pressed myself against the side of the boat. Between the darkness and my position, I knew that I would look like some sort of shadowy bundle. Yes, now I was poised for a secret; I cultivate them from a position of anonymity. Publicly I maintain the appearance of boring naiveté. I am the person that people do not notice, of whom they are never afraid; I have no power.

Those voices drew near to me. Even from my hiding place, I became alarmed. What if I were discovered? What could I say? My whole body clenched tighter; my legs were cramping. It was Hadrianus and Antinous, and they were approaching, standing next to me. I was afraid that they would hear the blood pumping wildly in my ears. I contracted like a stone in the night.

"Antinous when we get back to Alexandria, I'm sending you back to Rome and then to Bythinia. You will have a comfortable sum of money, enough to make you one of the first citizens there. I will of course want your discretion."

The barge creaked as it shifted on the mooring, and then all was silent until another voice slipped into the misty night. "My lord how did I displease you?" The voice began high and sweet and then cracked into a deeper male complaint. "I have been faithful to you, I have believed in you as no one else. In my life I have never felt such happiness as being at your side...the adventures we've been on, how you taught me to track game that no one else could find, and those moments with the goddess at Eleusis when we saw eternity together...even when you've been sick and failed, some part of me wanted to hold and comfort you."

Again there was silence. How strange to think that Hadrianus was out their, listening. How little he listened to any of us; we were all too busy plying the winds of his pleasure to care. Perhaps this was how these two spoke when there was no one else around. I heard Hadrianus' body shift. Did he touch Antinous? "You have grown up, Antinous. You couldn't be the boy-god forever."

"My lord but you too have grown...older." The way Antinous said older sounded like a challenge. How could that dear boy have used THAT word to the emperor? For an instant I almost wanted to cough or make some disturbance to stop what was happening. Maybe I could have thought of something clever. As much as the dear boy was utterly useless, still I did not want him to be hurt. Fortunately my ever-ready discretion won out and I stayed silent in the shadows barely breathing.

There was a petulant tone now to Hadrianus' voice. "If you mean the adventure with the lion, why I was only testing you."

"Then why did you look so scared when you missed? You were trying to run away. Even with that stupid poem of Babilla's, I know what happened. Everyone else does too; they're just too afraid to say it."

"How dare you talk to me that way! When I found you, you were just another one of those little tarts. I taught you to be a man."

"You taught me to be a man, and now as I become that,

you send me away. I never wanted to be a god. They may never grow old and die, but they never learn anything either. They're like spoiled children. You are trying so hard to be one of them that you're barely a man anymore. What you did on the deck tonight in front of your simpering audience was the act of a fool. I have tried so hard to keep respecting you. You keep playing these silly games. You're just fooling yourself. You never listen."

I heard the sound of Hadrianus gasping. After a silent minute his voice sounded sharp and bitter. "The truth comes out, you have been flattering me like all the rest. You all think that I don't know what's going on, but I do." His foot, inches away from me, kicked the side of the boat. The thudding sound echoed out into the night in forlorn complaint.

Was the god Hadrianus at a loss for words? Was his divinity frustrated or even worse sad? In my lifetime I had never imagined him to be sad. Gods can be joyful, randy, angry, benevolent, jealous, even petulant but never sad. That's for humans. It is the emotion of the second rate, of those who have to bow their heads to some power above them. Though I seem servile, I am never sad, just very careful. My little secret is that I am more intelligent than all the rest. In my cleverness I tower over them, all of them (Not that I am about to let anyone in on this, especially our dear emperor).

"My lord, I'll follow you forever, to the edge of doom; just don't ask me to pretend like Pedanius. He is too craven to look up at the sky let alone know anything about the stars. He's taking you for a fool."

There was a moment of icy silence. The the voice of Hadrianus rang out with hysterical rage, "I'm sending you back tomorrow! I don't care where you go, just never let me see or hear from you again." His rapid steps clipped i across the deck to his cabin in petulant rage. The night shattered, then became silent.

When my blood finally stopped pounding in my ears, I felt this bizarre and foolish instinct to slip out of the shadow, to say a simple word of caution or perhaps comfort to the boy. Not that I would have wanted anybody to see me, after all I have a career, but I remained hidden, reassuring myself that perhaps tomorrow I could find some secret way to be of assistance to him, yes tomorrow would be the time, ever so discretely; no one need know what I had heard.

I watched the dark shape of Antinous, it was absolutely still. There was something inside me welling up, perhaps just river mist, that seemed to make my eyes water. Did Antinous have that far away look on his face that once drew me to him? Did he see his future? I kept my uncomfortable position and turned my head away from him . I subdued whatever was rising within me. After all, he was unnecessary now and even dangerous. If truth be told, he was just another boy. The boat was gently rocking now: another boy, another boy, another boy.

Off in the distance a pencil thin edge of moon peeked over the horizon. I watched it gradually widen and bulge into a red angry ball as it rose. I heard the sound of a dog howling at that hateful messenger of night. My whole being tightened around that clumsy emotion rising within me and squeezed it like a fist.

I could not take my eyes off the moon as it rose swollen, free from the horizon. It silhouetted a bedraggled palm tree that reached across that sickening orb in crab like complaint.

That is when I heard the sound of something slipping into the water. I felt the boat beneath me bobble for a second as if it had suddenly released a burden, releasing it into the river. Then the boat quieted into a regular rocking. I watched the moon edge just a little higher. Then I heard a moment of churning and a brief splash; I held my gaze on the moon. Finally I heard a little clinking sound from somewhere, like a bell, and I knew whatever had happened was now over. I cautiously lowered my eyes to the river to see the last of the ripples broadcast themselves over the watery reflection of the moon. Antinous had disappeared into the depths. I have no words for the next moments; they could have been days or weeks or even lifetimes. The urgency to do something slowly subsided like some unruly disturbance of the stomach. That urge to act became a niggling irritation, and then that too rippled away leaving, I would like to say, relief. After all the dear boy was beyond help or hurt now, and there really was nothing I could have done. All in all his disappearance was a necessity, something of a foregone conclusion. My witnessing it was incidental.

I do not know why I kept sitting there when clearly all danger had passed. My body felt inert and empty as a shell as if something had rippled out of me leaving me strangely bereft…how absurd. I was at the apex of my career.

Someone stirred in one of the cabins. Quietly I stood up, my cramped body aching. I had survived again, yes… yes. Besides I had a slippery secret now, how lovely. I stood alone in my private darkness. How I love the darkness. The moon, my only witness, and it was small and silent high up in the sky now. I stood up and quite casually walked back to my tiny cabin."

CHAPTER 33

Julian stands on the wedding barge mumbling and shaking in a cold sweat.

Antrinous looks over at Hadrianus. "We were never alone, never. None of us ever are."

Hadrianus tears his eyes from the brilliant reflection. "Do you want a life with these wretches? Look at any of them, scheming, willing to give up anything if they get frightened enough or are offered some foolish prize. Look at them!" He goes over to Julian grabbing him by the back of his neck. Hadrianus drags Julian over to Antinous, slamming Julian onto his knees. He sold you to me like some kind of unwanted pet. This is the man you are living with!"

Julian looks up frightened, trembling.

Hadrianus' voice is softer now, pleading. "Is this the life you want to lead--wretched, aging and bitter? Look!"

Antinous stares at Julian's contorted face.

"This pathetic wretch only saw what a pathetic wretch can see, only understands what a pathetic wretch can understand. I love you with an eternal passion, a deeper, more powerful passion than any of these contemptible creatures have ever felt. My boy, my beautiful boy!" Hadrianus motions with disgust toward Julian. "What has he ever done for you? When has he ever been truthful?"

Antinous looks confused, torn--his eyes are slowly drawn to the brilliant image on the water.

"We need to get away. This is our last chance, last chance for a splendid eternity." Hadrianus holds the phoenix amulet around his neck. It is a shining pulsing beacon. He holds it out to Antinous. Together we'll join eternity, you my beautiful boy god and I your creator."

CHAPTER 34

Julian tears his eyes from the images in the water. "There's no place like Rome. There's no place like Rome. There's no place like Rome." Why did I say that? And why were all those masquerading fools looking at me? It was not my fault that that wedding was such an idiotic idea. Kneeling there I seemed to be flushing hot and cold and my stomach...oh my stomach. Finally the crowd turned their eyes away. I was able to stagger to my feet; I hate people seeing me when I am not at my absolute best.

Words and faces and sky were all rippling in waves of nausea. It was all I could do to keep a stiff upper lip, actually to keep both my lips stiff and oh so tight, stemming the tide of chaos that could spill out of me. It must have been the delirium, but I thought I heard Mother's voice gently whispering to, "Let go, let go, let go." It chanted irresistibly.

"Oh shit! No!"

Both Antinous and Hadrian had placed there hands on the railing of the boat. Even with the fog, I could see the eastern sky begin to glow.

Hadrian whispered longingly in Tony's ear. "Come with me into the floating world where everything is perfect."

Antinous glanced in my direction. Was it a goodbye, a reproach or even a last confused plea?

There was a pause as early morning sounds and light were beginning to seep through the fog around us. Truly wretched, I stood there suddenly not caring what anyone thought of me, an emptiness, a strange kind of emptiness, busy man that I was and am, I had never experienced haunting emptiness. Quite suddenly I knew from out of somewhere or nowhere that I couldn't let Antinous jump again. I know I am a wretch. I see it, I hear, I feel it. My whole gut is roiling with contamination, but somehow it doesn't matter; nothing matters except…letting go.

Then things became very simply, nothing heroic. I could feel the pressure bubbling up my throat, and into my mouth. Thinking of Mother, my mouth opened into a perfect "O," a kind of horrible orgasm building to the point of no return. I let go, something inside my self propelled a fountain of vomit into this world, this world that I wanted to be so perfect. Poor Babs she was standing close to me.

The image in the water of the Magnificent Hadrianus seemed to bellow a terrified guttural roar. He closed his eyes and slumped onto the deck. I saw Tony kneel down to cradle Hadrianus' head.

As I finally caught my breath…after one last throbbing convulsion, I noticed a little strand of mucous, laden with raw pork, dangling from my mouth and onto my toga; for the slightest moment I see how that strand catches the morning light and glistens in beauty.

I heard some old men laughing on the deck totally nonplussed about the chaos around them. They seemed to be playing some kind of game of chance, dice perhaps. I heard one of those ancients say, "Here today, gone tomorrow.... here again." Their cackling laughter rose in a crescendo, piercing the morning.

CHAPTER 35

Jerome and Cleo lay together curled up on the bank like two puppies. The morning was rich in sounds: birds, whirring traffic, even a few screams from the boat below on the river. Mother stood next to them watching and listening, wide awake.

Jerome stirs, wiping the sleep from his eyes like a child. He sits up, his face transforming into a mask of anger shoving Cleo away. Cleo wakes, her innocent face becoming a seductive mask.

Jerome stands up looking at the chaos on the boat below. "How disgusting! How pagan!"

Cleo glances at him. "You're such a fucking prude!"

Mother watches them quietly and then begins sorting through her cart, pulling out a newspaper. She opens the rattling pages, looking for something.

At the sound of the rattling paper, Cleo glances at Mother.

Mother starts reading out loud, "Italian Stallion, ex military man, veteran of service in the Middle East, looking for a voluptuous queen who needs a real man. Prefers dark eyed beauties with attitude. Let me rock your world." Mother smiles tenderly at Cleo. "It's your turn now dear."

Cleo blanches.

"You remember Mark…"

Cleo nods slowly, solemnly.

Down below on the boat on the river Adrian, his head on Tony's lap, is waking now.

Tony gently rests his hand on Adrian's forehead.

Adrian opens his eyes and whispers, "You were the only one who ever cared about me. I was supposed to be the hero who makes everything right this time, not just some bit player. Who would ever love me like this?"

"My dear Adrian, my dear fleeting Hadrianus. The story was never important."

"I don't understand, I don't understand how it turned out this way." His voice is beginning to sound young and petulant. He startles, jolts awake and looks around in wonder and then irritation. Suspiciously he stares at the old man cradling his head. "My name's Adrian…Adrian.

Tony silently witnesses the metamorphosis.

Adrian's features freeze into an expression of outraged contempt. "Get your hands off me. What are you some kind of faggot?"

Tony quietly releases the head and moves back.

Adrian stands up, waving at the young men around him. "Let's get out of here." He leads his bedraggled legion down the gang plank. When he reaches the shore, he seems to notice the amulet around his neck. Pulling it off violently, he tosses it into the grass.

Tony watches that figure take long powerful strides up the river bank and out of his life.

Sabina looks bewildered, waking from a nightmare. She

anchors her eyes on Babs. "What happened? What's going on…why are we on this boat?"

Babs quietly looks at her and then at the chaos on the boat, nodding her head thoughtfully. "It's just…it's just…" She is at loss for words.

"I had a strange dream…something Roman…I was getting married on a boat." Sabina looks down at the boat. "It was a dream, wasn't it?"

"A dream." Babs smiles, "Yes a dream."

"What is that terrible smell…why are we here?"

"Do you want the short or long answer?"

"Perhaps the short, you need to get out of those soiled smelly clothes."

"After much confusion, things work themselves out."

She looks bewildered gazing at the confusion around her. "I don't understand what this all means."

Babs gazes at her. "That's not as important as you may think…the words, I mean.""

CHAPTER 36

I watched Tony...he had a look on his face, open and innocent staring out like a babe looking at the world for the first time. It reminded me of something that I could almost remember, but no matter how hard I tried, it was just beyond the brink. Oh well, maybe for just this once, to be somewhat imperfect is not so absolutely terrible (not that I would mention this to anyone else but you. You will be discrete won't you?). Tony looked so dear in all his amazement; it almost broke my heart.

As the wind tickled my exposed chest, I realized that Tony and I were alone now on the ship. We should, post haste, make an immediate departure to the safety of the Murphy Hall men's room. After all what would passers by say if they saw me dressed like this?

But I had this strange feeling inside, not exactly warmness, but it was something. I decided that perhaps just this once I could take the risk of exposure...I walked over to Tony. Not that I had anything to say, after all he's not particularly bright and so often misses the import of what I say. Still, I had this unusual urge to hold him, my dear man.

I stepped up to him. "Why Antinous you look positively beautiful in that outfit of yours!"

He turned his gaze from the far off disappearing form of Adrian…now why did I call him Antinous? Like I discretely told you at the beginning of this story…I have been slipping of late.

Tony looked at me for a moment in disbelief; then an extraordinary relief filtered across his face. He seemed positively glad that I was at his side, even amazed.

I must have been hanging around Sabina too long or even worse around that looney family of Tony's; I felt something like deja vu, as if Tony and I had been on a river before. How strange, but there I was. My arms opened as if by my body's own intent.

I had the odd sense that I was forgetting something and looked deeper into Tony's bottomless eyes for a clue. How absurd to look to Tony for illumination, after all I'm a resourceful man who is always right…or at least most of the time. Why should I feel that I, Julian Scribner, was forgetting something? With just the faintest flicker of mischief, Tony walked into my arms. I felt tears on my naked shoulder. For a moment standing on the river I spun down into dizziness, but we held on as if we were saving each other's lives.

We both watched Mother come down the bank. Near the river she seemed to notice something in the grass and picked it up.. She stared at it as it sparkled in the morning light.

Did I tell you (I have been forgetting things so) that a week into the new semester, shortly after that strange event by the river, I collapsed in one of my classes; I just collapsed. When I woke up, I was lying in a bed in a hospital, tubes running in and out of me, machines pulsing in the brilliantly lit room. I demanded, demanded to know immediately what was going on. My students would be missing my lecture on ancient hygiene and plumbing.

A very sheepish looking young doctor came in the room to explain that I had some kind of brain tumor, a little seed of chaos had somehow planted itself in my brain and had been growing tentacles of disorder throughout my body. That certainly would explain all the strange things that seemed to have happened around me, even in side me.

Tony came into the room at that point and simply rested his hand on mine, listening. For some strange reason, despite the chaos inside of me, I relaxed just a little, almost letting go…so strange. At that point, Jerome and Mother peaked in. They said Cleo could not come that day; she was finishing some job. I did not know that she worked, but good for her.

For me the prognosis really is not good. Now that I am back home for a while, I have checked my diagnosis on the internet, and indeed…but I don't want to get into that right now. Did I say that I was home? It feels like home. A nurse comes in every day, Tony cooks for me, although my days of eating food are ending. I don't even mind Jerome's preaching. You see no one can threaten me with death anymore. Cleo has popped in a few times with her new man friend. I suspect he has a drinking problem. Mother comes by and just sits with me. I am loosing track of time; I can't tell if she is here for a few moments or a few eons.

But it does feel like home, not a solution to a problem, but just a kind of (I don't really have a word for it…imagine not having a word for it)…so very, very strange.

THE END

www.ingramcontent.com/pod-product-compliance
Lightning Source LLC
Chambersburg PA
CBHW020110310726

48970CB00002B/568